FAREWELL, GHOSTS
a novel
NADIA TERRANOVA

Translated by
ANN GOLDSTEIN

Seven Stories Press
New York • Oakland

SEVEN STORIES PRESS
140 Watts Street
New York, NY 10013
www.sevenstories.com

Library of Congress Cataloging-in-Publication Data

Names: Terranova, Nadia, author. | Goldstein, Ann, 1949- translator.
Title: Farewell, ghosts / Nadia Terranova ; translated by Ann Goldstein.
Other titles: Addio fantasmi. English
Description: New York, NY : Seven Stories Press, [2020] | Translated into
    English from Italian.
Identifiers: LCCN 2020017378 (print) | LCCN 2020017379 (ebook) | ISBN
    9781644210079 (trade paperback) | ISBN 9781644210086 (ebook)
Classification: LCC PQ4920.E767 A6713 2020 (print) | LCC PQ4920.E767
    (ebook) | DDC 853/.92--dc23
LC record available at https://lccn.loc.gov/2020017378
LC ebook record available at https://lccn.loc.gov/2020017379

College professors and high school and middle school teachers may order free examination
copies of Seven Stories Press titles. To order, visit www.sevenstories.com or send a fax on school
letterhead to 212-226-1411.

Printed in the USA.

9 8 7 6 5 4 3 2 1

For the survivors

"I always had the impression that we were a strange family, neither rich nor poor, much richer than the poor and much poorer than the rich, with a garden that was like a garden for the rich but a dark toilet where fungi grew."

NATALIA GINZBURG, "Childhood"*

_____

* Natalia Ginzburg, *Infanzia, in Un'assenza. Racconti, memorie, cronache. 1933-1988*, edited by Domenico Scarpa (Turin: Einaudi, 2016).

One morning in the middle of September my mother called to tell me that in a few days work would begin on the roof of our house. She said it just like that: "our." But for some time I'd had another house to take care of, in another city, a house rented by me and another person. The house I would have called ours no longer existed, that label had been removed when I left, and in the following years I had wiped it from my memory with thorough violence. Yes, I knew that the roof was falling down—it had begun to fall down when I was born, and had been crumbling, raining down in the form of dust and flaking plaster, for all the life I had lived there—but I wasn't in any way responsible, we can't be blamed for the things we don't want to inherit and have already disowned. I wrote fake true stories for the radio that had had an unexpected popularity; I had a man, a job, another city, new evenings, and a different time.

My mother said that she had had to deal with every problem by herself; she was tired now and the house was a burden to her. Redoing the roof, which was flat and tiled and functioned also as a terrace, would be her last act of generosity—because certainly she couldn't put the house on the market with all that damage—before buying a smaller and more solid place. She said that a contractor would repair the holes caused by bad weather, poor insulation, and the neighbors' old renovations, while in our house—she repeated: our—under the roof, under the feet and labor of the workmen, she and I would sift through furniture, utensils, and books to begin to empty it: she didn't want me to be able to reproach her one day for giving away my things, and so I had to return and choose what to let go.

I thought it would be easy, because, apart from a red iron box kept at the bottom of a drawer, I didn't care about anything.

I packed a suitcase with a few clothes and some underwear, and bought a train ticket on the Internet for the next day: I would look out the window for the long stretch of sea beside the Calabrian railroad all the way to Villa San Giovanni; from there I would take the ferry to Messina, bringing my mother the help she'd asked for.

That night I dreamed I was drowning.

My husband's foot, propped against my ankle, warmed the bed, and at some point I began to move from the warmth under the sheet into the water.

I was walking as if I knew where to go, and the water cooled ankles, calves, knees, and then thighs, hips, belly, breast, and shoulders, and then chin and mouth, until I tried to speak and immediately disappeared, swallowed up by a wave. A moment before, I was walking; a moment after, I was drowning. My sight didn't dim, and my strength didn't evaporate, only this thing happened: I entered the sea and in an instant my body no longer existed.

I woke and sat up. In a whisper, I called to Pietro, my husband, not because I needed him but because I didn't want to keep from him the fact that I was dying. It seemed important, dying, and I wanted him to witness it. My arms and armpits were sweaty, sweat dripped across my forehead and shoulders, he grabbed me by one elbow and, with an effort, opened his eyes and sat up next to me. There was nothing we could say to each other that would console me, and I felt unable to share either the burden or the fear of my dream.

Once, more than ten years before, when we'd been together only a few months, I reproached him for having so little interest in my nightmares; when I was a child my paternal grandmother urged me to tell them—if you don't tell them you won't be free of them, she said—and now that she was gone, if he didn't ask I couldn't tell, and wouldn't be free of anything. So at night when I woke suddenly, and in the morning before going to work, Pietro had begun to ask how I was: Tell me what you dreamed, he insisted and insisted, and I tried to answer, but it didn't work. Things never work when they're transported from one era to another, they're fine where they are, and there's always a reason that memories should remain memories and not come to disturb the present. I had been wrong to tell him about my grandmother: in her big bed with its scent of fine old sheets, the account flowed naturally, whereas opening myself to him was an effort. It was the same that night, too, neither of us had a desire for words; it was an agreement we'd made long ago, as long ago as the times when we responded to fear with desire, to nightmares with sex.

I grabbed the plastic water bottle from the night table and took long swallows. My husband touched my back with the sort of love we had then, a weary love, made up of hands that, never too intimate, caressed the stomach around the belly button, desperate hands that gripped the edge of a T-shirt, the elastic of underpants, a love that seldom became something else and pushed beyond, spinning in circles of static affection and splitting in two by itself, withdrawing after a brief illusion and letting us return to being two very separate entities. I drank and swallowed and Pietro took my arm, I lay down, and he lay down, too, I turned onto one side and he turned first toward me, spoonlike, and then onto his opposite side, and finally we rubbed against each other, back to back, to rock ourselves and try to go to sleep again. Struggling to follow me, even sleepily, was his way of loving me, the way people can still love each other after ten years. At a certain point our bodies had stopped functioning together, stopped fitting together in sleep and the waking that precedes it; we had become shields for one another.

Sex is a language, and many words had been uttered between Pietro and me in the early days of our relationship, when I was running away from Sicily and from a family that was maimed and full of silences, and he welcomed me in Rome, becoming companion, parent, brother. So, along with the city, I found a new self, and he was there, always there, and that availability was moving. In those first months we took off our clothes as soon as we could and after having desired each other to exhaustion we were happy, even though one detail might have warned us that it wouldn't last: we never made love twice, the first time satisfied us, and immediately we began to separate and get dressed. Everything we sought we managed to give each other in a minimum time that never expanded, after which we reestablished our singularity, the separateness that had also been our rule of attraction. But soon—too soon for a romance that claimed to be the romance of a lifetime— that separateness became an enemy. The body stopped being the place of communication. The sweetness was poured out in daily rituals, in dialogues and kindnesses, and even if we fought during the day we never really hurt each other: we lived each in the shadow of the other, each watching over the other with a care I'd never known; after desire ended we had developed a ritual for giving each other pleasure anyway, then, after a time, that exchange, too, became unusable, like an old dictionary.

The fault, I knew, was mine. It must have been I who closed myself off first, unaccustomed as I was to openness, to sharing.

But to Pietro, and only to him, I had told the story of my father and he hadn't raised questions, he had accepted the anomaly. We had known each other for three weeks and neither of us was much over twenty, when on our first real date he showed up with a package: inside was a blue skater's T-shirt and a diary with a hard cover. At that moment I saw in him the man I was waiting for. He didn't know that as a girl I had skated for long hours, he didn't know that I had written a lot about myself in various diaries hidden in drawers. And yet he knew.

So I confessed to him that my father had disappeared when

I was thirteen. Not died, just disappeared into nothing, I continued, waiting for the question I feared: Didn't you and your mother do anything to keep him?

But Pietro never asked that question. He asked nothing, listening attentively to the few sentences I was willing to concede: my father, a high school teacher, had left the house one morning and hadn't returned. And then he changed the subject. He said that the work I was looking for at a secondary school would be wrong for me: the lives of others, of students, parents, and colleagues, would overwhelm me, and I would soon find myself enslaved and unhappy. He didn't say that lives don't repeat and that it didn't make sense to follow my father's, to become a teacher like him: he had put the emphasis on something else. The crowding in classrooms and halls wouldn't give me any respite; I should write, instead, and put into my stories the pain that couldn't go elsewhere.

Until that moment Pietro and I had always met on happy occasions, and thus I discovered that my eyes exposed that pain, and I was convinced that his capacity to read it was outside the ordinary. On that conviction I had based our life. Day by day I relied on him, his seriousness was a rock and, like all rocks, had walls that could be difficult, hostile, to climb. Sometimes I said to myself that I wouldn't know how to make an appointment with the dentist by myself and wouldn't pay bills or taxes if I didn't know that I would put the receipts in the folders he had organized for the apartment we rented. Being together every day, making every decision together, knowing by heart the smell, the sex, the character of the other: that was marriage. The rest was a stormy, unknown sea, and there was no point in crossing it.

I felt my husband rubbing against my back for five, ten minutes and then he fell asleep again, while I stayed curled up toward the wall, hoping not to have to confront the water again; the night hid weapons for my defense, but I had already used them up. I was becoming invisible again, while if I drowned, if I died, I would have wanted Pietro to see me.

The counterpart of the darkest fear is an unexpected lightness: I wanted to make love as if we could devour each other, as in the early days. I turned and began to caress him impetuously, but from him came a sound that interrupted the rhythm of his breathing, while his body contracted defensively. We could touch each other and cradle each other, but the possibility of making love made us retreat like terrified animals: it would mean having not more intimacy but less, losing that little physical closeness that with difficulty we had gained. We knew each other too well to challenge our reticence to see each other naked, a view that allowed neither of us to let go, not because we didn't find the body of the other beautiful or attractive but because we would no longer know what to say or how to say it, now that that unused dictionary was sleeping between us.

I also withdrew, onto my other side, and again turned my back to him. I took his hand and put it on mine near my belly button, brooding with my eyes open. I thought I was grateful to him for that advice ten years earlier. In my fake true stories I put part of my pain and the water that overflowed from the past, and I hoped that writing would be enough to save me, but then came a murmur, a disruptive voice suggesting that gratitude wasn't enough to keep a marriage from drowning.

So in the insomnia that had no end, between my sweat, Pietro's regular breathing, and fear of a shipwreck, I waited for a dawn that would never arrive. But everything arrives, sooner or later, destroying the people we were or think we are: at the first light of the sun I got up silently, kissed him on the lips, and went to the station, leaving him asleep.

PART I

The Name

We Nest Only in Dirty Places

Driven by the crowd that was disembarking from the belly of the ship, I passed through the Caronte company turnstiles and found my mother. She was wearing a light, short dress, above the knee, and had let her hair grow to her shoulders; her face, in spite of the sixty-eight years that ought to have marked it, was self-conscious, like a girl's; her slender body was placed between me and the island, forming an entrance to the city. I noticed that in growing up—aging—she had begun to resemble me, as though she were the daughter. She smiled at me with a candor that once had been mine: so I hadn't lost it, I discovered, only left it as a legacy to her. She asked me how the trip was and why I'd taken the train rather than the plane, but for me it was normal to get on a train in Rome, wait for the sea to be visible from the window, get out at the station in Villa San Giovanni: to cut the Strait in two in the September light, rejoice in the crests of waves stirred by the sirocco, huddle on the bridge among strangers who, smoking, were looking out over the parapet, choose a point between Scylla and Charybdis and hold on to it with my eyes for the whole crossing. The crossing: one reason the return was worthwhile.

The sun lit up the plastic sign of an abandoned supermarket: "Welcome to Sicily," lights burned out for a decade, greeted me, and quickly and in silence we left the harbor area. Amid streets dedicated to sea myths, Via Colapesce and Via Fata Morgana, the house awaited us. It was only an ugly extra story added on later to a nineteenth-century building, a plastic crown on a real queen; its decline was recounted in the vestiges of ornaments on the surviving balconies, a lion with undulating, flaking mane, faded and discolored symbols of nobility, dilapidated green-painted wood shutters. We had lived there together for more than twenty years, from my birth to the day I left for Rome; childhood and adolescence had remained to watch over the house like swallows, whose wings I heard beating out of season, while my mother rummaged in her purse for the keys. Every spring they made a nest in the façade of the building across the street; afternoons as a child I spied on that agglomerate of black threads from behind the shutters, and mornings, just leaving for school, I immediately looked for one like it under my balcony. With the fierce instinct of children I felt that spring was the season of death, of earth rotting under the celebration of flowers, but I wished to be part of that deception and its scents, and I prayed that a swallow would choose my house as its personal point of transit. Why don't the birds stop at our house, I protested, getting in the car, and my mother, distracted, more engaged in putting the car in reverse than in soothing me: It's better that way, they nest only in dirty places.

I turned back to her and she found the keys.

"What are you thinking?" she asked.

"You remember Dollface?" came to mind, and she laughed.

That was what we called the neighbor across the street, a man with the round, placid face of a doll who spent afternoons on his balcony, above the nest that the birds were constructing, a nest he knew nothing about. He went through the day ignorant of the animals that were busy under his feet. Thus my mother and I arrived at the house as three: the old complicity of one of our nicknames had placed itself between us, a creature only she and I saw.

Entering, I smelled the dampness of the walls, mixed with the odor of dust. I thought of my husband and held on to his image: he was still at work, already tired from the day; I should have sent him a message to let him know I'd arrived.

Suddenly the house summoned me to itself.

The room where I had slept, played, studied had remained fixed over time; floor and walls were occupied by the magma of objects exiled from the shed on the terrace, which my mother had emptied before my arrival. A dead room, invaded by waves of memories.

"There was no space in the study or the living room, they're covered with flaking plaster," my mother explained, in the imperious tone of people who refuse to be in the wrong.

In fact, in the other rooms a flood of white plaster dust had been deposited on couches, chairs, and bookshelves. In mine, instead, the life we had accumulated together was poured out onto the furniture and the floor. We nest only in dirty places.

I sneezed.

"The dust has always bothered you," my mother noted.

"That's not true, I became allergic when I moved away from the sea."

When I left Sicily, my nose was the first thing that changed. It had grown more and more congested, hostile and scornful toward the scant oxygen of the capital, saturated with cement and smog; then my skin had changed, because of the chalky water that came out of the faucets and the exhaust from the cars; finally my back had changed, curving unnaturally as I got on and off buses and trams. Thus I had been Messinese and become Roman, had been a girl and become an adult and a wife.

"As long as I was here my breathing was fine," I insisted.

In my mother's eyes a grim satisfaction appeared; meanwhile I was tired and getting sleepy, so I asked if we could have dinner early, and afterward, finally, I shut myself in my room alone.

With every movement, a fine dust rose: from the pale wood shelves when I grazed the spines of the books that filled them, from the pillow and the framed prints I ran my finger over, from the pink cloth bedspread I moved aside to get into bed. The mattress was too small; to be comfortable I would have had to cut off my feet at the ankles. The idea made me smile; I lay down, avoiding pillows and sheets. I couldn't have had any memory of many of the ages that surrounded me, but I knew the story of the wicker basket they'd brought me home from the hospital in when I was born, along with the legend of the blue wool blanket given by a cousin to celebrate my birth; my mother despised this cousin because of a dull, stocky boyfriend, with short fat thighs, who—she often repeated with a gesture of disgust—had come to the hospital in a leather jacket, and, since she had just given birth, that vulgar odor of the secondhand had nauseated her. My mother, accustomed to project onto objects what she thought of those who had touched them, adored the basket and hated the blanket; between the first, sitting on the floor, and the second, on the night table, I would have to seek my place for the night.

There were still old clothes of mine in the drawers, I pulled out a T-shirt and closed my eyes, so as not to feel the assemblage of all the things.

First Nocturne

I wake with mites in my lungs. Anxiety or asthma, I shouldn't have agreed to sleep here, returning is always a mistake. Dust or sea air, I can't breathe, I went to sleep too early.

I'm a grown woman pinned to the darkness by her childhood dolls. Other families would have kept one, at most, in mine we've kept them all. The one sitting in the basket, in place of my newborn self, blinks in the dark.

My classmates' houses were so light that when I entered I imagined they would lift off from the ground; the owners had the freedom to leave them at any moment, while my mother and I struggled to walk in ours, chained to the objects we didn't throw away. We kept everything, not to celebrate the past but to propitiate the future: what had once been useful could be useful again, you had to have faith in objects and never absentmindedly throw them away. We saved them not to remember but to hope; all the objects performed a role and launched a threat, and now they're around me, looking at me.

The striped waterproof playsuit from when I was three, put away for the children I haven't had. The trousseau and the tarnished silver and the chandeliers wrapped in white cloths, for married life and the apartment I didn't buy in Rome. The girls' boxing gloves, which lasted for a few exhausting lessons in a rubber-floored gym, until I understood that I'd be trained for everything but defending myself: at most I would learn not to suffer from being the weakest. And dozens, hundreds of objects of every shape and size, puppets, books, colored plastic toys, wooden combs, boxes of clothes: I saved and submitted to the will to save, I hoped and submitted to the will to hope.

The room is now saturated with unused hope.

Through the shutters comes a puff of wind, the sirocco has grazed the dry leaves of the aloe on the balcony that died in the heat. If I close my eyes memories are staged on that balcony.

One. Peeing on the plants, one night when I came home drunk after a bonfire on the beach with friends, because I didn't have the energy to cross the hall to the bathroom.

Two. At dawn I heard the sound of horses in the street, I thought I was dreaming that a coach or carriage had gone by; on waking I told my mother, who nodded but didn't believe me. As I discovered, looking out one night, the sounds belonged to clandestine races: the delinquents from the adjoining neighborhood closed the streets and transformed them into a mafioso *palio*, where people flocked to bet on underage jockeys and moribund horses. My fragile neighborhood, stuck between the middle-class apartment buildings of the center and the working-class projects on the hill, invaded alternately by one and the other, was born and grew up apologizing for its anonymity. I close my eyes tighter; that is an ugly story.

Three, fear. One night after I'd decided to leave, and was nearly done with my packing, I went out on the balcony to smoke. A sound of footsteps in the street made me look down: a boy in a hooded sweatshirt, hands hidden in his pockets, stopped, looked right and left, squatted down suddenly to leave something under a car, and ran away. The neighborhood, at that time, had been colonized by small-time dealers, who took advantage of the fact that, because of the burned-out streetlights, the sidewalks were always dark. I went inside, closed the outside shutters, the inside shutters, the curtains, exaggerating the fear: I was afraid that if that kid had looked up and seen me on my balcony he would at the very least have murdered me, and consoling myself, I repeated that I would leave, leave, leave.

Four. There has to be a fourth memory, I hope it's slight. No use. Night brings proximity to stinging memories, insomnia, and desperation. It might help to think about sex, if I could concentrate.

Sleep returns along with my mother's commands. Don't go out on the balcony, it's dangerous, we'll have to deal with redoing the façade soon, too. It's not your problem anymore, I answered, avoiding her future, since you've decided to sell.

The White Light of the Strait

I woke with the heat and voices of the morning, and looked for Pietro's foot; sticking mine out into the space, I remembered that I was in the little bed, was alone, and hadn't yet written to him. My husband and I didn't like to talk on the phone when we were apart; we'd made a pact not to intrude on each other, to act so that our lives, once they were distant, could take different routes, all possible routes. "Good morning," I wrote, sleep making my hands sluggish, as I tapped on the phone with half-closed eyes. "Everything fine here, hope so for you." The lack of a question mark was the signal: You're not obliged to answer, I know you're there.

On the street, two floors below, a motorbike with a broken muffler was slowing down, a girl was calling someone in a loud voice, from the balcony opposite came the sound of carpets being beaten in the sun. In the room the light absorbed the excess dust, the outlines of objects became fixed, thoughts returned to order. The memory of insomnia

27

got me up immediately, frightened: it was better not to delay, not to stay imprisoned in bed after such a difficult first night.

I crossed the hall barefoot, in my underpants and the T-shirt I'd slept in. In the kitchen, a sheet of graph paper was stuck in the spout of the coffeepot on the unlit stove, bearing my mother's prescriptive writing and the imperative of a single word: "Light." Passing her room, I had glanced in and seen that it was empty, but I didn't need proof; I knew very well that we were alone, the house and I.

Whenever I stayed alone in an unfamiliar apartment, I moved in a state of paralysis, cautiously obedient, under the severe gaze of the absent owners. If they had told me to take off my shoes, I walked barefoot, if they were afraid that something would break, I didn't even touch it, as if they really could reproach me for violating their rules. Mindful of how tense this made me, I tried never to be a guest, and when I traveled I always chose anonymous hotels, beds with carmine quilts and panoramic watercolors over the head-boards, neutral, uninvasive rooms, to which I could bring my nightmares and my insomnia. I sought relief in being alone and yet I never was alone: as far back as I could remember I never had been, especially in the house in Messina. There, until I was thirteen, my solitude had been inhabited by my mother's parents, who died before I was born: we had inher-ited the house from them, and it took them a long time to resign themselves to leaving it. They reappeared once a year, on the Day of the Dead, but I had the impression that they were always watching over it, even in my most embarrassing moments, when I was in the bathroom, or lost in secret fan-tasies.

In that same kitchen, Sara, the friend of my adolescence, had told me she had had sex with two boys at the same time; by then our bond had nearly dissolved, we were approaching one of those inevitable separations that mark friendships before adulthood, each the other's witness of years we're ashamed of and would like to forget; that afternoon, one of the last, when neither of us was quite eighteen, I envied her for what I would never have had the courage to do. I was sure that if I tried to have fun, the dead of my family would reappear at the foot of the bed to stare at me in silence; the dead are envious judges of all the actions they can't perform anymore, of the errors they can no longer commit, of the entertainments of the survivors. My mother's dead had remained in the house with the precise intention of knowing me, the granddaughter born after their passing. My grandfather, anticipating his own stroke shortly before it arrived, had brought the car to the guardrail and died on the highway, with the four emergency arrows flashing; my grandmother had developed cancer a few months after her husband died, and the house had thus ended up in the hands of their only daughter, my mother. The old people came back to see us the night between the 1st and 2nd of November, when I set bread and milk out on the table and the next morning found the milk half drunk and the bread half eaten, as well as an envelope with a banknote, the hard pure-white almond cookies in the shape of the bones of the dead that I gnawed on, hurting my teeth, and the marzipan fruits that were left uneaten, because they were nauseatingly sweet, and just looking at their perfection was enough to satisfy: sculpted and colored to resemble a prickly pear, a bunch of grapes, a slice of watermelon. That it was my mother who put on the clothes of the dead and performed the fiction didn't matter, didn't make that nighttime passage less true. That was death as I'd known it up to the age of thirteen: a straight, infinite line that had to do with heredity and the inescapability of time, a place people don't return from except once a year for a celebration, an unfortunate but essentially fertile event. That's what it was, and it didn't frighten me.

Then one morning my father disappeared.

Not like my grandparents, already old before I was born, not like an accident or a heart attack that ends a life. Death is a full stop, while disappearance is the absence of a stop, of any punctuation mark at the end of the words. Those who disappear redraw time, and a circle of obsessions envelops the survivors. My father had decided to slip away that morning, he had closed the door in the face of my mother and me, undeserving of goodbyes or explanations. After weeks of immobility in the double bed, he had risen, turned off the alarm, set for six-sixteen, and left the house, and he hadn't returned.

At seven-fifteen I got up for school—I was then in the last year of middle school—and I went to the bathroom to wash, crossing the hall as I had done since I was born, as I crossed it still as an adult: underpants, T-shirt, bare feet, and three-quarters of me still snagged in the night. On the kitchen table was the milk and the biscuits, but passing the bedroom I had felt an absence (the insufficiency of a place, its not being enough: not even the room-prison had been able to restrain him). For a long time my father had huddled between the sheets, with the psychic grief no one talked to me about, but I intuited a lot. I knew that he was there, and that after school I would pretend to have lunch with him; I knew that he wouldn't eat and I knew that I would give my mother and myself a different version of the facts. But in my not-looking that morning was a perception of irrevocability.

I've often wondered if that wasn't a story I invented later, adding what I discovered in the afternoon, that my father had gone, but that false sensation would still have been truer than the truth. Memory is a creative act: it chooses, constructs, decides, excludes; the novel of memory is the purest game we have. Coming home, I noticed from the street the new furor that animated the house, I heard it as soon as I turned the corner, like my mother's crying. My mother was calling my father's name, and as soon as I entered she attacked and suffocated me: Your father has gone, your father has left us. And even though at the police station they told us we had to wait seventy-two hours to report his absence, she didn't want to wait even a day to report to me what she knew, what we both knew: a depressed man had consciously and forever left life and the two of us.

So at thirteen I became the daughter of someone who had disappeared: the real dead die, are buried, and you weep for them, while my father had vanished into nothing, and for him there would be no November 2nd, no calendar—he would no longer have one, and my mother and I wouldn't have one, either. That year we didn't celebrate the dead and the grandparents didn't come to see us. In compensation, on November 2nd precisely I got my first period. As for the house, it had become the sacred place my father might return to at any moment, and now my mother wanted to sell it. What would become of him, alive or zombie or ghost, the day he showed up at the door, reclaiming his half of the bed and his place at the table?

The smell of burned coffee brought me back to the present, and I fixed my eyes on the kitchen wall, the only wall of the house adjoining another apartment. In the past a noisy family of evangelical Christians had lived there; at night my mother and I heard them through the wall, singing, while, unmoving on the couch, like part of the furniture, we stared at the television, gripped by our fiction of placidity, as if there had always been only the two of us, the two of us period. They're singing, I thought, staring at the TV news. I forced myself to imagine seven people around a table concentrated on praising God, brothers, sisters, a mother, and then that other adult, the father, the word that was now so painful.

"You burned the coffee," my mother said, entering the kitchen with a bag of vegetables.

I thought: My father disappeared twenty-three years ago.

"I got the coffee ready so you just had to turn it on."

I thought: He disappeared into nothing and after the first days we never talked about it.

"I put a note in the spout the way your grandmother did with me."

I thought: Why didn't we talk about it anymore?

"Have you been up long?"

I thought: Why didn't you talk about it anymore?

"The workers are coming at eleven for the final assessment."

I thought, looking at my legs under the T-shirt: She's telling me to put something on to cover myself.

"Have you started choosing what you want to keep?"

I said: "You mustn't touch any of my things."

Twenty-three years have passed, I thought. What have I done in those twenty-three years, where have I been, who have I listened to. There could be beside me a stranger of twenty-three born the day he left, and beside her the child of thirteen, stopped forever at that age. I looked at the girl, I looked at the child. The child wasn't growing up. She would never grow up. She would continue to stare at me, motion-less, the whole time I was in the house.

"They're here!" my mother called from the door.

I put on some green cotton pants that had once belonged to a gym uniform and looked for a mirror to straighten my hair. I found a shard of rough glass with the drawing of a flower on the side. I'd painted it with my cousins, and then we set up a stand on the seaside road to sell things. We sold perfume bottles belonging to our mothers, aunts, grand-mothers, a few mirrors, bracelets—all dusted, washed, and decorated by our adolescent hands. At that time I carried in my chest a burning, unexploded grief, a small red-hot sphere.

Looking in the mirror, I smoothed my hair with my hands, shifting it to the side, and the telephone vibrated. "How's it going?" the screen asked. "Let me know when you can." I seemed to feel the roof collapse another little bit.

I put the telephone under the pillow and left the room.

In the front hall, a boy of twenty and a father of sixty were talking to my mother. "Signor De Salvo," she introduced them with a smile, "and this is his son Nikos. The mother is Greek."

The slight intoxication in my mother's voice suddenly made us all exist: me, them, the walnut prie-dieu, the umbrella stand covered with plaster dust.

"Greek, interesting." Throwing words together randomly I led that father and that child toward the hole in the living room. "Greek from where?"

After more than two decades, another father was entering our house, employed by my mother. The small sphere began burning in my chest.

"From Crete," Nikos answered; he bumped into a pile of old board games in a corner and Snakes and Ladders fell on the floor. "Watch out," I got angry as I followed the pieces that rolled under the chairs, and we bent down to pick them up. "Wait, I'll do it." I had used *lei*, the formal "you," and he had responded with the informal *tu*: I would never learn to impose the authority of hierarchies.

Meanwhile the father explained to my mother the difference between thermal and acoustic insulation and my mother answered that we didn't have a noise problem, only a water problem. Nikos and I, once the last piece had been picked up, closed the game box.

My mother was lying about the noise. After my father disappeared, during the long afternoons at home I heard a child shoot a glass marble against the walls, wait for it to come back, shoot it again, so that it rolled along the floor, and start again. At first I thought it was one of the children of the evangelicals, but the noise wasn't confined to the common wall; I heard it sometimes in the hall or the bathroom. Years later, in a puzzle magazine, on the page devoted to "things you might not know . . ." I discovered that the specter with the marble infested various houses in Italy, and was in reality the gurgling of old pipes.

"We'll take care of getting rid of everything," Nikos said, pointing to the Monopoly set I'd loved in elementary school, and then: Clue, at which I often beat my mother, discovering a certain talent for suspecting the right people; Snakes and Ladders, in which I'd moved four pieces, imagining I was playing four different contestants; the puzzle of the Picasso painting depicting a girl with a dove in her hand; and, finally, my favorite game, Scarabeo, with the stands for the plastic letters that you then arranged on the board, composing new words. During the last Christmas with my father, we had all three played, forging ever longer words and trying impossible ones, and when we got to the final round the order was: me first, my mother second, my father third. Then my father had written "locomotion," and when he won, beating us, his eyes lit up, a rapid blue wave raised by the wind.

"I'll take care of deciding what we throw away and what we don't—you have to work, there's a lot to do," I said brusquely to Nikos.

Meanwhile my mother and his father were agreeing on a schedule: every day from seven in the morning until five in the afternoon—if possible even later, they shouldn't waste time as long as there was light, shouldn't lose time when it wasn't too hot for the heavy jobs. I noticed that Nikos had a long scar on his left cheekbone. Neither he nor I felt the need to add anything before saying goodbye. Children know how to be silent.

Once we were alone, my mother and I had lunch, without

much conversation. ("How is it that Dollface occurred to you yesterday?" "Who?" "Dollface, the neighbor." "He liked you, Mamma." "What are you talking about?" "He was out on the balcony for you." "What do you mean?") Then, as soon as the sun allowed, we went up to the roof and in the evening light I looked around.

Here was what surrounded the house: the terraces of other buildings, old antennas, drying racks with sheets hanging on them, clouds stretched until they frayed, the archaeology of ships docked in the port, the military port coiled on itself and guarded as a pruning hook, the outlines the same as they had always been: faded, sleepy, distant. And me: the child who waited for Sunday to go up to the terrace with her father, opened the shed door, took out the little red car, and pushed on the pedals, whipping right and left between tables and swing. He stood still, hands in his pockets, my mother leaned out over the parapet, looking at the sea and waiting for the return of something we weren't allowed to watch. There were no traces left of that world. The terrace was stripped of everything, and after the work was done even the last memory would be banished forever.

"Nothing will change, only the floor," my mother said, guessing my fear.

I squatted down with my back against the outer wall of the shed. The roof was falling down, and it was still the most beautiful place in the whole house, in the entire city, in fact in the whole world. Maybe that's why it was falling down: out of shame and shyness. The white light of the Strait was a marvel, more rarefied than the fog, touched by the September sea and by the palm leaves infected by the red palm weevil epidemic.

"It's got them all," my mother said. "All, a damn disaster."

We stayed on the roof while the light changed from white to blue to darkness, we spent an hour, two, the voices rose from the street, sometimes insistent, sometimes faint, an entire symphony at our feet. They talked under us, they swarmed in the street that kept changing, they talked in our place; if there was an art in which my mother and I had become expert during my adolescence, that art was silence.

Every night at dinner, vehemently putting a fork down next to a crisp burned chicken, a salad of tasteless tomatoes, soups too salty, carrots and soft processed cheese, chicken livers and canned meat, complaining because the refrigerator had frozen the drinking water and the oven hadn't warmed the food, my mother and I wanted to demonstrate to my father that we had made it. Even today we don't speak of you, we reminded him, with the napkin sliding under the chair out of weariness, and no wish to retrieve it. Then, having ordered him to stay outside the boundaries of the unspeakable at least for the night—exhausted, in our care-lessly donned pajamas—we went to bed.

We did the same as soon as we came down from the ter-race, at the end of my first day at home: we said good night with a kiss on the cheek, like the girls we had been.

The morning my father left the house and didn't return wasn't over yet: inside me the clock had never signaled afternoon. At lunch I followed the border between life in the midst of others, at school desks, and life at home, and that border was: roulades of meat in the oven, packaged lettuce, yogurt, and mozzarella. After I cleared the table, time inverted its direction, and in the afternoon the rooms became a forest, the hall a canyon, the study an ocean. I arrived at the desk, opened the Greek dictionary, climbed up on the chair on my knees, and began to translate.

Only my friend Sara violated the house. She came over to study as soon as her neighbor went out, leaving the dog unattended, an old female who barked out of nostalgia; that whine crashed through walls and ears, Sara said, while at my house silence reigned. She sat next to me and we did homework until it was late. Someone, therefore, found refuge in our house, considered it welcoming, that it had its charms, although my father had once described it as the worst place he had ever lived, and I was convinced of that, too, an apartment out of scale, an excrescence sheltering furniture accumulated at different times, the pale-blue paint peeling in the corners. The long hall ended in a grandfather-clock case; no one had had the time or will to install the clock machinery. Then, a year after my father disappeared, my mother stopped to look at it and said: The clock, we should have put the machinery in before. It was the thing most like the name of my father that she had uttered, and I envied her for getting so close, closer than me, closer than I was then capable of. In what had been my father's study, four plywood boards resting on red bricks, like a bookshelf, were still occupied by Hebrew, German, French dictionaries—there was no language whose alphabet and phonetics my father hadn't begun to study, only to abandon it right away. And then the books on information technology, medicine, mineralogy, every branch of knowledge he had intended to learn in the last years in which, as a concession, he had continued living with us: the reflections of Seneca, the folly of Erasmus, South American poetry, essays on Soviet politics, an illustrated book on the earthquake in Messina in 1908. After he left his job, and before he disappeared, my father read in order not to hear the sound of his unhappiness, until the effort must have become insupportable to him.

His absence watched over us on afternoons of studying; Sara and I didn't touch his books, we would rather have bought new ones. We were girls who were blindly trying out a friendship: I wasn't anyone else's friend and never could have been; I revealed no hint of the nightmares that infested my sleep, my eyes were dry, enlisted in a rigid form of resistance. I was guilty of my father's disappearance, because, I thought, it was with me he no longer wanted to live. I was the one who had taken care of him in the last period, when my mother left the house to go to work (we can't afford to lose my salary, too, she said), and every day she departed with the same phrase: I'm not worried, because you're with Papa. I was the guardian of my father, therefore guilty of his flight.

The first day of high school Sara sat next to me. My father had been gone for eight months, and, exiled from the middle school class where I'd felt like someone with the plague, I thought my guilt was so enormous that it had been transmuted into a deformity, a repulsive physical defect.

Right after my father's disappearance I didn't go to school for several days. When I returned, none of my classmates named him and no one asked questions; besides, no one had ever been to my house: with him depressed and always in bed, I didn't have friends and I never talked about my family.

In high school there weren't the old classmates, there weren't witnesses, but still the other students all had a father and a mother, living or dead. Maybe some of them had read in the newspaper the story of my father's disappearance: there is nothing more frightening for a teenager than entering a new class and suspecting that someone may know something about her and won't speak to her about it.

Sara came toward me smiling, with her freckles and her long blond curls, and asked: Is this free? As if anyone else would really have been able to occupy the place next to me. I had been grateful to her, as ten years later I would be grateful to my husband: I formed my bonds out of gratitude toward those who perceived my abyss. At the start of my friendship with Sara, I imagined I heard her neighbor's dog crying at night, and I would have liked to imitate it, if someone had taught me how to do it, if my father had died, like others, and my mother had been able, like a widow, to teach me the gestures of mourning.

That didn't happen, and every day my father disappeared a little more.

In the morning, dawn illuminated the peeling paint of the old wood shutters, my mother said we needed different ones, aluminum, more durable and shiny. She repeated it, and meanwhile we kept the old ones, which were superior and needed to be maintained, she and I who knew no conjugation of the verb "maintain." It must have been because of our untidiness that my father had left, it must have been because of those days when he was fading and we didn't know how to hold on to him, because of those blankets that never seemed to protect him sufficiently from the cold, our incapacity to make him accept the doctors' prescriptions; meanwhile, my father's name was hidden in the water, in the leaks and mold on the roof, and at fourteen I spied from the windows the sea, the ships, the traffic, the outline of the palm tree drooping in the rain.

Afterward, my mother and I had lived alone in the damp house and had never been successful at being alone.

My father's name remained on the dinner plate, was hidden in the fruit rotting on the sideboard, on the wall a gecko slid by, my mother cried that the mice had returned, the tablecloth danced and the forks and knives banged into one another, I stopped up my ears until the noise passed. My father's name tyrannized us: when we gave it respect, it mocked us, departing for weeks, and leaving us enclosed in despair and fear, but if we applied ourselves to forgetting, it came out of the refrigerator, out of the drawer where his medicines had expired, planted itself in front of the table set for a meal; the man who had been my father looked at our life and would continue to do so forever. He had infiltrated the pipes that we hadn't repaired, sat in his place so as not to leave it empty, laughed at the shame with which we ate our lunch. My father monitored the house like a guard and had abandoned it like a coward: both things continued to happen every day, a tired afternoon rite, and evening was used for finishing homework, turning on the television, and staring vacantly at the commercials.

Do you think he's dead? my mother asked, and beyond the walls the balconies flooded, while not a word came out of her mouth or mine. We said instead: The edges of this frittata are overcooked; Mamma, remember the Latin translation: I got a seven-minus; Tomorrow I have to buy new seat covers. We also said: Killing geckos brings bad luck, are there more? And we meant mice. One gecko, one alone, hid behind the cherrywood cabinet in the kitchen, it came out on hot evenings, paying no attention to us, and we paid no attention to it. Sara had told me that she'd found a nest of mice under her sink, they preferred damp areas, nothing odd if they had invaded my house along with the water. At her house, her father had killed them. At mine, I had.

Between sunset and dinner, my father's absence came back to visit me. I opened the door to the balcony hoping that the storm would seep through the ceilings and tear open the cracks in the wall, I begged the north wind to become a hurricane and overturn the clock and the chairs onto the floor, toss the bed, the pillows, the sheets in the air. Don't you want to know that I grew up, doesn't it interest you? I asked, and no one answered. My period stained sheets that in the morning I hurried to scrub with white, fragrant laundry soap, spread on the back of the dish sponge.

Little by little, my father had habituated us to his coming departure; like everyone he had begun to die the day he was born, but at a certain point he had decided to cheat that disintegration, and he must have felt omnipotent going down the stairs that day, closing the door behind him with a cordial goodbye to me, to my mother, and to the smell of moldy water that arrived in his place, in the form of steam and gusts of wind. Disappear, choose a point in time and close the trapdoor behind you, forget people and things, since the west wind would erode memories as violently as it persisted in cracking the walls.

Papa returned today, too. My posture at the table confessed as much to my mother: the bent back, the weary gaze that girls shouldn't have had dropped into the kitchen from the mistaken universe of existence that goes on. He was here a moment ago, did you also see him? shouted the speed with which I finished dinner, in order to get out of his sight as soon as possible. Instead: No, thank you, I don't want anything else, Wednesday they always show the same film, I wouldn't be late for school if you'd buy me a motorbike.

Meanwhile the telephone, placed on a pile of trousseau linens, informed me: four messages. Not enough to mean that my husband was so alarmed that he would break his habit of not calling me, but enough for me not to delay writing to him. I thought again about our habit: we lived according to the idea that two distinct people existed within a marriage, one plus one, near or far, stuck together or separated, but always two, never one alone. We'd lived that way from our first day together, avoiding fusion: two columns that bore the same weight. We believed that separating without questions was a way to stay together longer than passion or symbiosis would allow; in our marriage, endurance, duration were an end, not simply a means. We wanted to be together forever, and for that reason were careful not to become sated with one another. I thought back to our last night: both my dream of water and the bed where our marriage was drowning in the absence of desire were far from Messina. When we were apart Pietro and I became two monads again, two jellyfish, each pushed by its own current. Traveling, we respected the life of the other, without jealousy or bad thoughts: crossing the border would have meant failing, and we didn't want to fail. During the day we managed not to collapse, but every night we failed. In one of my fake true stories for the radio I'd written about a couple who had stopped having sex: they were young and were alarmed; I had given him a physical problem and her a nervous complaint, and I had managed to come up with a happy ending. I knew that Pietro would listen to it, he always listened to my program. Two nights later he came over to me as if to collect a reward, as if he had arranged that encounter; he had lowered my pajama bottoms and we had made love like strangers, silent and vengeful.

I looked at the screen.

My husband had written: "Everything OK?"

And also: "A registered letter arrived, I opened it, it was what they owed you for last year."

And also: "Sure you're all right?"

And also: "Don't make me worry."

This time the monads were not completely detached, the jellyfish weren't swimming in opposite currents. My husband had felt that this trip was different, he knocked, he asked. I thought instead that it would be better not to let him exist during the time I would spend in the house, I thought that no one should have to exist outside my nightmares or my memory.

Before going to sleep I apologized in a hundred and fourteen characters: "I'm sorry, the house is in worse shape than I thought, it will take me a while, but I'm fine, and so is my mother."

Second Nocturne

I'm walking through whiteness, and not far away is my mother, her head hidden by a red hat and scarf, walking with a woman I don't recognize. Half sunk in the snow, in a pastel T-shirt that leaves my arms bare, I greet both of them and laugh, I laugh loudly, until I run my tongue over my teeth and they fall out, one after the other. Confused, I look at myself from the outside and see the mouth of an old woman, with no more defenses, a mouth emptied out and inhabited by scars. With an implant, solid and artificial, in place of the premolar. And also, the mush of decayed incisors, canines, premolars, and molars, smells of saliva and medicine, there must be blood. I look at myself reflected in the report of my orthopantomogram. Teeth: misfortune. Cats: gossips. I have to wake up. Teeth or snow? Wake up, wake up. I wake up in a tired light.

I've been wearing the same shirt for an entire day, I wad it up and throw it away, it lands near the balcony. I get up and put on a clean one and go back to bed.

Six-Sixteen Forever

"Yes, wait, do you need water? And for the boy, I'll get it cold from the refrigerator."

"No, signora, we have water, but could you come up for a moment, we need you to look at a piece of wall near the cistern, because we can't knock it down without your permission."

"I'm coming, I'd like to bring my daughter, but she's sleeping."

"You know the saying: A father provides for a hundred sons and a hundred sons don't provide for a father."

Eyes open, burrowed in the bed. My new day in the house began with the sound of the bell, the voices of my mother and Signor De Salvo.

I would relinquish the respect earned for getting up early, and not seem a reliable and present daughter, but I wanted to be alone and no one would prevent me, the house and I had been apart for a long time and I couldn't predict how much longer we'd spend studying each other. Besides, my mother had summoned me not to help her out with the work but to sort through the objects: that was the task I was responsible for.

Nikos must be on the terrace, already at work, with his clinging T-shirt, sleeves rolled up to his shoulders, calf-length pants plaster-stained, calves in work boots. It was eight o'clock, and soon the sun would give us no escape; the sun of September is a misery, it's egotistical, mournful, and outsized. People who know nothing about Sicily think that the light brings good humor and spread that misconception about cheerfulness, but Sicilians avoid the light and endure it, like insomnia and illness, unless it's a choice, and no one can choose light every day of the year. It would blind us, disable us. Even light can be an enemy.

That half-Greek boy should have put on a hat to shade his scar; I was worried, even if it was no longer new. He and his father were above my head demolishing and destroying and later, perhaps, would reconstruct the cover of the house; I would see them trample my tiles, stick their hands in my things—that "my" surprised me. My things, I thought, while I knew I would lose them, some or all.

I looked at the drawer where, under a pile of diaries, I had saved the red box, the only thing I was interested in keeping. I would deal with it at the right moment: opening it could hurt me, I wasn't ready yet.

Meanwhile, I would feel the breath of those two men, the alien closeness, the smell. If for Nikos I felt an instinctive sympathy, I couldn't say the same for his father: he was only slightly younger than my mother, and the way he looked at her hadn't escaped me. I covered my chin with another edge of the sheet, and that gesture left my feet uncovered; the cotton protected me from the mosquitoes and the heat, from the sticky duties of daughter, heir, owner, and from every role that fate had chosen for me. I concentrated on the red box, as if its existence could expel the rest, and imagined for an instant, only an instant, the moment when I would reopen it.

"Don't worry, it's fine like that, call me if you need me."

"We'll be making noise on the kitchen side, I'm sorry for your daughter."

"She has to get up anyway, sooner or later."

My mother's footsteps stopped in the doorway. She knocked. I imagined her opening her mouth to call me, instead she had the wisdom to say nothing; when I heard her go away I looked at the clock that had long stood on my father's night table and now emerged between a modern lamp and a knot of electrical wires. It always displayed the same time.

That morning twenty-three years earlier my father had opened his eyes at six-sixteen, and the numbers remained on the alarm clock, switched off with a sharp stroke, six hundred and sixteen, six one six, and for days his blue toothbrush had sat on the sink, lying outside the glass where we all kept ours, trailing a wake of toothpaste like a snail's slime. My mother had already gone out, as she often did, to treat herself to a long walk at dawn, before going to work.

Before it was six-sixteen forever my mother would walk for hours every morning along the coast and then return to open the regional museum, where she sat at a narrow desk, like a nursery school desk, welcoming the tourists who disembarked from the cruise ships. Messina didn't deserve a stop of more than half a day: French, English, and Americans passed through with sandals on their feet and cameras around their necks. Few ventured as far as the museum. My mother, at night, told us their stories, described what they were like, what sort of couples they formed, how many children they carried on their shoulders or in the stroller, what part of Europe they came from. My father taught Latin and Greek at a private school where rich kids who were repeating grades got a diploma bought by their parents. The school was named for an architect and set designer from Messina: "Filippo Juvarra Remedial School" said the plaque; my father, incapable of remediating himself, remediated others. Every so often a student who was more diligent or less rich came to our house in the afternoon because he needed an extra lesson, specific drills to avoid the second or third failure. My hair tied in two perfect pigtails, I hurried to welcome gangly adolescents ("the beanpoles," my mother called them with resigned detachment) before skating back to my room. Skating in the hall was allowed, skating was always allowed; my father wanted me to take part in certain regional contests and watched my progress with satisfaction, praising it excessively. Whenever he could he trained me, saying that I was almost ready, almost perfect.

Then the days had been transformed into a single day.

My father had left his job, my mother had extended hers infinitely; he stayed in bed sleeping, she invented any excuse to go to the museum.

The bed where once my parents had loved each other, had conceived me, had been happy and young, had become, with my father's depression, his room.

My mother had begun to place my father in my care, along with countless orders: Cook the pasta, don't overcook it, make the coffee, no more than a cup, don't fill it, like that it's not enough, take it to him in bed, try to make him get up. No student rang the bell anymore. All the rooms stayed open so that, suffering from sadness, he was never alone, and in the silence I could converse with the small sounds, the rustle of his pillowcases, the pen I dropped on the floor, the ring of the telephone—so I tried to inhabit the day, a land increasingly bereft of human voices.

Our world (might there exist another one?) had gotten stuck.

The last months my father spent with us were a lava-like and muddy material, a toneless mood that enveloped everything. I was thirteen and didn't know how young you are at thirteen, how grown-up you think you are; the fairy tales you leave behind don't warn you, don't deliver a legacy of tools. What are the warnings that a kingdom is about to end? My father got out of bed only to go to the bathroom, he had stopped eating, speaking, smoking his pipe.

When he finally disappeared, sleep went with him. I arrived exhausted at school in the morning, horns honking in my ears, yawning, too; families were packed into SUVs stopped at a traffic signal, standing in the bakeries buying pizzas, adults saying goodbye to kids in the school court-yards, parents enduring the abandonment of children like a private exorcism: See you at one, we're only pretending to leave each other. The same game, the same courtyards where my father came to get me when I was in elementary school. At that time I knew that after the sound of the bell I would find him outside, one hand in his pocket and the other drumming four nervous fingers on the unmoving thumb. His name, alive in the mouths of friends, was uttered, followed by a greeting, and my father turned and picked it up like a thing fallen from somebody else's pocket; he exchanged the greeting and, spinning around, took the school bag from my back and shifted it to his. Then, lightened, I grew a pair of wings, and all the way home I'd have my back covered.

Soon after my father left, when the outline of his body was still fresh in the bed, I dreamed about him for the first time, twice in the same night. He was climbing up the pipes in the courtyard to the kitchen balcony, disheveled and in his pajamas, having just gotten out of bed in another house from which he'd escaped with the light of remorse in his eyes. I opened the shutters, breathed the morning air. Get up, let me in, he laughed, forcing me to welcome him back; I woke up screaming. My mother was sleeping in what had been their room, careful to keep me and the rest of the world outside the door. I had gone back to sleep and my father appeared again, he was swinging, legs dangling, in the empty space of the courtyard, tied to the grille by a sheet around his neck, hanged, as in the game we played devotedly, with paper and pen, in the hot afternoons: either you guessed the secret word or you died. He was wheezing and, in a murmur, asked me to help him or let him go. For the second time I opened my eyes with my hair stuck to my forehead and the fear of not breathing, in the limbo of insomniacs there was no escape. It was still dark, but for me the night ended there.

Later, some acts of force by which I held on to my father's name. At night I waited for the clock to display our time, six one six, to find his odor of tobacco and talcum powder. In the morning I walked the streets of the city with my neck tense, eyes low on the cracks between the bricks, small white squares squeezed together to form new ones, a field of luminous squares turned gray by the shoes of the passersby. I looked up and concentrated on the people, I recorded their features and wrinkles, weight and lightness of pace, the speed with which they got in and out of cars, I spied on the neurosis of greeting, shoving, purposely ignoring, I unearthed feelings suffocated by habit or repressed by convention. I knew every centimeter, every person, without recognizing anyone, because to recognize is to feel at peace, to fit into the city like an appliance in the kitchen, while I was never at peace and in the middle of that army of faces I saw only the absence of one. To go to my friend Sara's I had to pass near the cemetery and on the way I held on to my father with greater arrogance. I crossed outside the stripes, dodging moving cars and the barricade that separated the graves from the city, I tightened the straps of my backpack, I skirted the kingdom of the dead where my father didn't live and walked like a stranger on the streets of the living, because he didn't live there, either. I arrayed my line of defense around the perimeter of the cemetery without fearing the counterattack of ghosts, I strengthened my legs and nurtured thoughts of revolt. One day, I said to myself, my father would return and show the world who we were.

But when I started high school, I had a short journey in the morning: I cut through Villa Mazzini and greeted the *Ficus macrophylla*, the witches' tree; there was one in Piazza Marina in Palermo, which I'd seen and photographed during a school trip—it was older and bigger than the one in Messina, but it wasn't mine. Finally, at the end of a back street, on the façade of the high school, was a saying from the Fascist era: "Thirty centuries of history allow us to look with supreme pity on certain doctrines that are preached beyond the Alps." A hundred centuries of nothing fell on me, the load of books, notebooks, pens dumped into the backpack from elementary school to adolescence with no one helping to lighten my load anymore; I wondered what sense there was in urging us to be sad and superior, to remain entrenched in pity. Why should I have to take refuge in history when, at fourteen, I wanted only to free myself from it? Since I could no longer have wings, I was owed a free, unencumbered future. But the black strokes of Fascist calligraphy on the wall were contemptuous, and didn't answer.

When it rained, it rained in my shoes. My father's name, decomposing into watery exhalations, coincided with the annoyance of wet socks and soaked my feet with mud, fine cotton surrendered to the apocalypse. A few drops aren't enough to stay home, thundered the teacher, equal parts cruel and friendly, whom I struggled not to call mamma, she knew so well how to mix authority and dignity, and so great was my need to have more than one. Because of a few drops of rain we have seven absent, does that seem normal to you, she insisted, roaring, and at least I was proud of being there, after crossing the city like a hero, whereas Sara's half of the desk was empty:

she had dry socks and both parents, I had a desperate victory over the fury of winter. But I couldn't hide the gullies in my family, they appeared in hair made frizzy by the storm, I dried the lenses of my glasses on the edge of my shirt, I lowered my gaze to the teacher's mauve boots, damp at the back, her pale stockings, the tip of the umbrella left to dry next to the desk. My father's name pounded on the windowpanes, from Dante's Inferno came Acheron, Styx, and Flegethon, the rivers of the damned, in silence I prayed that no one would discover the true cause of that flood, I, I and my damaged family.

My mother and I didn't know how to repair the damage and so we lived it.

My father's disappearance had become the funnel of our guilt, the headache of choices to avoid.

Our family, lined up and mutilated, was forced to go forward until it was torn apart by a platoon of white soldiers. It was the black pieces, always the blacks, that I hid behind after dinner, placing the wooden chessboard on my father's side of the bed; my mother moved the first pawn two squares, I came up with weak strategies, we continued to play, without an hourglass, until my eyes closed, until I took underwear and pajamas off the radiator where we'd put them so they'd warm up and protect us from winter, clothes burning like armor for colorless nights—finally, undressed from the day and armed with flannel, I cleared the painful half of the bed and, arms overflowing with towers and knights, went back to my room.

As for the game, she always won.

I raised myself on both elbows, and the bed got smaller; I would die devoured by objects, the alarm clock said six-sixteen, would say six-sixteen forever. I grabbed the phone, no message. Telephone time is real, only telephone time is real. Nine-forty-eight.

I wrote to Pietro: "How are you?"

And also: "I miss you."

Finally, prudently: "We're dying of heat, not a good idea for you to come."

Nine-fifty, minimal intrusions of air.

Three Centimeters

On the terrace my mother stared, frowning, at the workmen
on the job, father and son unstoppable, she leaning on the
parapet in a daisy-printed dress that left her back uncovered,
the skin darkened and thickened by summer. She glanced
at my legs to make sure they were covered to a respectable
length; a laugh escaped me, did she really think I was still
an adolescent who would go around half naked even if there
were men in the house? "You're so pale," she noted, coming
toward me. "You never go to the beach?"

"I cover myself—the sun's dangerous," I said, excluding
my husband from the answer.

The silence between us was filled with endless summers
made up of carrot lotions, bottles of lager poured on arms,
necks, calves, chamomile in the hair, and every herbal trick
that I, in particular, adopted to make my complexion less
milky and my hair less dark. As I got older I had begun,
instead, to protect my complexion, my natural colors.

Denying what you were, becoming something different and then forgetting you had wished it—there was no other way to become adult, or if there was I didn't know it. Thinking of the past as a line composed of various segments, each piece representing a girl who no longer existed but had once existed undeniably, a daughter who had left and had married a man and new habits, in another house and another city.

"Signora, what to say, the problem remains the same," De Salvo said aloud.

"They insist they won't make the second drain, and here with a drop of rain we'll be flooded again," my mother whispered.

Then I realized I had interrupted a mute dialogue between her severe gaze and the back of an exasperated Signor De Salvo, who, with his hairy belly sticking out below the T-shirt pulled over his navel, was bent over the floor, sweating in search of a possibility only my mother saw clearly.

"It really can't be done. You would have to ask your neighbor to remove those three centimeters—believe me, with the second drainpipe we wouldn't fix anything. Or we raise the level, but at that point we'd have to be sure that they won't raise theirs more, otherwise we're back to where we started."

Three centimeters.

In that difference in level between our terrace and the neighboring one the story of our family was imprisoned, in that step the story of how my mother and I had survived, with an ostentatious superiority, Sicilian to the bone, a stubborn pretense that nothing was wrong, in the face of snubs, insults, pettiness, even more than injustices. So, rather than yield, it was better to go along with the misinterpretation of gentility, passing for a superior class of people who don't get mixed up in brawls, don't wish to be confused with trash. From then on I would always display my detachment, like a moat to protect the turmoil inside. But, to stick with the story of things, things had gone like this: one dull winter morning after my father's disappearance an injustice had erupted on the roof. It wasn't so much the three centimeters of reflooring, which suddenly made the evangelical family's terrace higher than ours, but the informal and welcoming aspect of the whole, a direct offense to us. In the space of a few nights and a few days the evangelical papa must have labored to create on the roof a second house for his nest of children, the double of a dollhouse: he had enlarged the shed, giving it doors, windows, and shutters, put up a water-resistant metal gazebo, covered the new tiles with succulents that would never die, encouraged an ivy to climb the fence that divided his property from ours, a slender young ivy that would let us glimpse the lightness of their days. Come and see, my mother had growled, leading me up the stairs, and, following her, I had left my Italian notebooks open on the desk. On the roof, facing our dilapidation, I had seen: a new colored plastic tricycle, pails, shovels, and an inflatable pool that would be filled with summer shouts, pottery vases, and tidy curtains ready to shut out winter. Do you realize? my mother fumed, they've raised it five centimeters, so when it rains the water will flow toward us and we'll flood. Five centimeters, she repeated with assurance: she had already gone up once to the terrace to measure. I saw, I tried to calm her, looking away from the whiteness of their blinds; I couldn't smell the odor but I was sure it was detergent, bread at breakfast, the scent of newborns and evening songs of praise. Happiness always occurs in other people's faces, the evangelicals wanted to be happy in ours.

From that day on, we talked only about the difference in level.

She was no longer at peace. Discovering that the centimeters were not five but three didn't soothe her, the water still flowed, a little more slowly but it flowed. Three centimeters measured my mother's hatred for other families, indifferent to what had happened to us. My father's absence had been transferred above, to the roof, while below a unique litany was performed: when the air became dark and electric, when the dogs barked and the palms rustled, the threat of rain made my mother nervous. She walked back and forth in the hall without looking at that single wall, I silently counted the first thunderclaps, and if with the first downpour the neighbors' youngest child began to cry, she opened the refrigerator and took out a yogurt or a cutlet that immediately slid out of her hand and infuriated her, because we couldn't go on like this.

"Signora, are you listening to me? I'll repeat it now that your daughter is here, the only way to keep the rain out of the house is to raise it three centimeters and make it level."

Time, meanwhile, had made the two terraces more alike than they'd been in the past. The dividing fence was now fragile and rusted, I stuck my right hand into the lattice and pulled it out maroon with rust, impossible to get your whole wrist through a square. It wasn't only my limbs that had grown; the entire roof seemed smaller. In memory our side was big, desolate, abandoned to the wind and the dust, the childhood toys piled up in the shed; the neighbors' half was just as big but friendly and full of objects. Now that both had grown older, their terrace was like a middle-aged lady who had been beautiful in another decade, while ours, sunken and destroyed, was preparing for a possible rebirth.

De Salvo stared at my mother, waiting for an answer.

It doesn't matter, we'll take the water, I would have liked to say, we've always had it and we'll have it as long as we live, it's all that remains to us of my father, does that seem outlandish to you?

In Sicily, the island without water, where you always have to reckon with drought, where there are fights over aqueducts and no one has yet found the solution to taps that dry up every evening, the water never left us in peace.

"You're right," I said instead. "You're absolutely right, Signor De Salvo, if we don't resolve the question you can't work. I'll take care of talking to the neighbors, so we can be sure they won't raise it again."

Third Nocturne (Afternoon)

I'm seven, I never sleep during the day, I want to play and not waste time. My mother chases me up the stairs, even if I don't sleep I have to go to bed—you're not allowed to disturb the adults' rest. In my entire childhood I fall asleep at most two or three afternoons, stomach down, head turned, mouth open, and drool on the pale cotton of the pillow. It happens to me again now, after lunch; after the promise I made to De Salvo, I'll talk to the neighbors, encouraged by my mother's icy eyes.

I collapse, and dream.

I get a telephone call while I'm driving the car, not on my phone but on an old walkie-talkie; in fact I'm following instructions from a distance, someone is leading me to the body of my father. I'm driving, yet I see the scene from the outside, as a map, a treasure island map; the car is moving with me inside and the walkie-talkie on the dashboard switched on.

I park, get out, sink my feet in the sand, men are digging, we're here not to bury but to exhume, the bust, the head come out, along with clods of earth like the ones that are thrown on a coffin, but there aren't any coffins, and all the movements are backward, from the earth to the surface, until a body wrapped in a shroud is hauled up, is it the body of Christ?

They've brought me here as a god, it looks like Palestine, they speak another language, they speak all together, but I don't want to participate in this thing that appears to be a banquet, I don't want to touch the bones of God, I don't know what to do with the bones of God.

I don't want to dig up the body of Christ, I want to dig up the body of my father. I want to hug it, whisper to it, shout at it, touch it, hug it again.

We're here not to bury but to exhume.

The Blue Hour

In the coolness of the afternoon I decided to go out. The De Salvos had finished work and would return the next day, my mother was in her room listening to the radio as she rearranged the closets; she was taking out the linens and organizing them by color, putting them back in the drawers according to new criteria comprehensible to her alone. The voice of the host was announcing a suite, the sound of the cello was resting on objects that suddenly were not too many or too invasive. On the landing I stopped, I hadn't yet closed the door, I went back and took the telephone out of my pocket, left it next to the alarm clock. Finally freed from time, I faced the city.

It was the hour when, on the Calabrian coast, on the other side of the sea, the highways and the overpasses stand out clearly, while on this side Messina spreads and rises again, descends into small valleys, and opens at the corners to stairways; it points at the sky with fountains and steeples, bows down from Catalan cupolas to broken sidewalks, looks out the windows onto working-class courtyards. It must have been after the earthquake of 1908 that we stopped throwing things out, historical memory making us incapable of eliminating the old to make room for the new; after the trauma everything had to live together, pile up, we could demolish nothing, only construct to excess out of fear, shacks and apartment buildings, streets and streetlights: overnight the city was there and then it wasn't, and if the disaster had happened it could happen again, infinite times. So it was better to train yourself to hold things together, put up a building right away to cast a shadow on the one before, then a third to take the view away from both, and so on until the architectural implosion became an inextricable tangle.

The only way was to walk along the sea. Walking, I would fight my battle, as when I tightened the straps of my backpack to go to school or to my friend Sara's. Away from home and objects, away from the front door and the usual street, away from memory and the empty grandfather-clock case, away from the alarm clock that had stopped twenty-three years earlier.

Now, on the street along the sea, I had to choose my direction. To the left: the shore and the museum; that is, the water and the place where my mother had worked for years. To the right: the cathedral and the entrance to the highway; that is, a historic center touched up like an amusement park, and the possibility of flight. But I wanted only to take advantage of an hour of invisibility, an hour without the telephone, without the clock, without pockets, without anything. I could go up toward the panoramic neighborhoods, choosing one of the streets called *torrente*, because the city had originally been traversed by rivers, which were then silted up to make roads that wound from the coast up into the hills. Torrente Trapani, Torrente Giostra, Torrente Boccetta . . . With my eyes closed I smelled the odor of fresh water poking a hole up through the asphalt, Messina was a city with a muddy foundation. I chose to go to the right, toward the *passeggiatammare*, the sea so mixed with the city you can forget it exists, like the rivers buried beneath the streets.

It was no longer day and not yet evening but, rather, the blue hour: no boundary between sky and water, the line of the horizon vanished, countless gradations of a single carpet of color. Clouds above the statue of the Madonna in the harbor, a couple of addicts quarreling near a bench: he shouts, You're a bitch, you're a real bitch, she shouts louder, Stop it, lower your voice, people will hear us. A few horns, waves against the cliffs. You're a bitch, you stole my soul; you're a shit, you still owe me the money from last year. There's something vital in the desperation of people who yell at each other, even chase each other, pursue a word, beg for a response; I envied that relationship, that attachment to life which I had had, and which then must have disappeared into the depths of the sea, along with the king's ring that Colapesce is charged with recovering. The myths of the Strait had been my fairy tales as a child, Cola who grows fins because of the time he's spent in the water, Morgana who charms swimmers when the air is too clear, Scylla and Charybdis, nymphs transformed into monsters; the sea that separates the island from the continent, that thin liquid strip

crowded with ships and, once, feluccas for fishing for sword-
fish—an insatiable sea, made fierce by the apparent calm of
its limits. It's not open, tourists and visitors think, seeing it
imprisoned between two tongues of land; it's not open, and
so it's safe and protected, they think. But what can't extend
outward sinks down to infinite depths, and the myths are
there to remind you.

Of course, to a superficial glance, that water is only a rectangle.

Alongside me a tram passed, a relative novelty for Messina. But two decades before, when the sidewalk was still
free of tracks, I had walked that stretch countless times in
my gym uniform, hair bound in a braid, with the anxiety
about running and sweating typical of slender adolescents.
Even earlier, in childhood, I had gone back and forth on that
sidewalk, from the day my father gave me a pair of roller
skates until the day I fell while he was distracted by one of
his mute thoughts, which wasn't unusual in the year before
he disappeared. Stumbling, I had skinned a knee, an elbow,
and half my chin, and my upper lip was swollen. My father
got up from the bench, shaken out of the apathy in which he
now passed his days, and said, Let's go, come on, what are we
doing here, these things aren't for us. I had unlaced the skates
and put them over my shoulder, setting off on the sidewalk
behind him. The cars passed us in the opposite direction,
my father didn't turn, he didn't hold my hand, he didn't
admonish me to be careful. I would have liked to admonish
him to look out for the cars and stay near the sidewalk, but
I could no longer tell him anything and so had kept it to
myself: Let's hope he doesn't die. I must have thought it so

strongly that, soon afterward, the gods had punished me by fulfilling that wish: my father hadn't died and never would.

We stopped going to the *passeggiatammare*: it wasn't I who had made a mistake but my father, who had discovered that concentrating on something other than himself was a luxury he could no longer afford. In the morning he pretended to open his eyes but he didn't really look at anything, my mother put the tray with coffee and a plate of sesame biscotti next to the bed, she went to walk along the sea and then to the museum, I left for school calling out bye at the door. What material my father's days were made of was a subject to avoid.

Things were the same only in my memory, and the same as they followed me out of the house; memory has sturdy shoes and implacable patience. I tried to leave the sea behind me, advancing into the city. On Via Santa Caterina dei Bottegai the windows of the apartments on the second and third floors were closed. No one lives there anymore, I thought, and right away: No, they must have gone out for dinner. Staying home at night at the end of summer was a mortal sin, they'd all gone somewhere or other to enjoy the cool air, they'd return later, families with children and couples in love, opening the windows to let in the September night, ready for bed or a last discussion in the kitchen. Imagining them, I managed to tolerate the deserted street.

Finally the contours of my high school appeared. Out of the last window on the lower left, our classroom, the teacher had hurled a trot found under a desk: it's better to know nothing than to have half-baked notions. I paused on the saying high up on the wall: "Thirty centuries of history allow us to look with supreme pity on certain doctrines that are preached beyond the Alps." Instinctively I glanced at my feet, but no: this time my shoes were dry, shiny, a pair of anonymous dark flats. A condensation of dampness in the air entered my bones. The blue hour had turned gray. But before going home I had an ultimate goal: the small square near the courthouse.

In the afternoon, when we finished our homework, Sara and I would go and sit at the Fonte dell'Acquario. Dusk descended on cars idling, bored, at the traffic light, and we sat on a bench with paper cones of smoking-hot *crocchette* bought at the nearby *rosticceria*. Sometimes we sang. Behind me I felt the breath of the marble boy astride the globe, sometimes he blew harder and warmed my neck with a palliative warmth, water never spurted from his fountain and I never felt like crying. Sara was like me, but intact, her house was light and ordinary, her thoughts free to coincide with her history. When we were together I, too, could be fourteen, so I held on to her like a shipwrecked person, I who had hated all ages since my father stopped having one and who knew that his every birthday would be celebrated against me.

The name of that place came from the god Janus, later Aquarius, or, for the people of Messina, Gennaro.

Now he was before me again. A familiar god, covered by weeds, small and more anonymous than the giant of my memories, not the boy who blew on me on the noisy afternoons of adolescence but a mute piece of marble without importance.

I lay on the bench, hands interlaced under my neck, knees pulled up, in the midst of the pierced hearts and quotations written with a felt-tipped pen on the iron back. The streetlights came on, and I no longer thought of anything. The past was a distant region, things are motionless only in my memory, the same memory repeats countless times like a theatrical début, my father wakes at six-sixteen, flicks off the alarm, and magically that clock doesn't go forward; he chooses a tie, puts down the tie, brushes his teeth, leaves a trail of toothpaste like a snail's slime, goes out of the house in the blue shirt, turns to look at the door, has a flash of melancholy satisfaction. Curtain, darkness, no applause. My eyes hadn't seen that memory and yet it had been playing inside me for twenty-three years.

I turned on my side. I took out of my pocket the only object I had brought from the house: a green pen with which I did my homework and wrote Sara passionate letters of friendship. On the iron back of the bench, among the names of lovers and vulgar, obscene drawings, I begged for the peace of a corpse and wrote the words that real orphans can afford to mock and survivors of a disappearance yearn for like tranquility: "Here lies Sebastiano Laquidara, his daughter Ida weeps for him."

When I finished writing my father's obituary, the fury of his name subsided.

PART II

The Body

Life Is the Blink of an Eye

My whole life I had been the daughter of the absence of Sebastiano Laquidara. While I was becoming an adolescent the house was damp, the winters windy and the summers dry: the driest one was the fourth after his disappearance. I had turned sixteen that winter. You'll be the prettiest sixteen-year-old in the city, my mother had promised when I was a skinny, scrawny child, and to honor that promise, or that anguished blackmail, my face became less hard, small but well defined, soft breasts developed. I wasn't pretty, but I was something else, my body had listened to my mother, or, simply, she had known because she had already gone through it: sooner or later everyone comes out of childhood, my mother had received the instructions before me, she knew how it worked. I emerged with difficulty from a compendium of protuberances—bony nose, teeth straightened with metal braces, pointy knees and elbows—and the mirror gave back a new image, the polished version of a possible aspect: mine. My mother had predicted it.

Day by day, as my skin stretched and my body length-ened, as I grew rounder, the climate became drier, and the vengeful absence of my father threatened to leave the people of Messina without water. It hadn't rained for weeks, the newspapers reported the water crisis, and the walls oppressed us; in the suffocating heat my mother and I hurried to buy two floor fans, placing one in each bedroom, mine and hers. All day, with my legs stretched out and tickled by the moving air, I read my books, not the ones on the improvised shelf where my father's handbooks were piled. At a bookstore in the city center I had chosen Albert Camus's *The Plague* because it talked about dead mice, and in the house I had flushed out the mice and defeated them when my mother was afraid; Camus's mice could be a metaphor for what-ever they wanted, but for me they were real, period, they reminded me of my struggle and my triumph. My mother would never have had the courage to set a trap, move the couch away from the wall to get at the hidden rodent, shout to frighten it, make it hesitate and fall onto the cardboard smeared with glue. Nor would she have had the courage to finish it off with a blow from the broom: these actions I had performed.

At night, sweating, I crossed the dark hall to the kitchen, opened the freezer, detached the few slender excess stalactites from the frozen food, and took that solid water to bed. I rubbed the pillow with ice and, having re-created an illusion of coolness, fell asleep again, struggling to turn over because the few extra kilos of my new femininity, compared with how thin I'd been in childhood, were weighty and burdensome; if I turned on my side I felt them, if I was on my stomach

I noticed. I was no longer androgynous and so: Who was I, what was I going to be? My mother had known in advance that I would change, I had to admit. I said to myself that it was a simple and common experience, I didn't recognize in her a maternal instinct, we were two trees planted at different times and she had grown first, that didn't make her a parent, just as being born later didn't make me a daughter, on the contrary: the more we grew, the more we were plants that happened to share the same terrain, if the small one wanted to observe the large one she had to raise herself up a little and twist, exposing branches and leaves to the risk of rain or sun.

While an entire region suffered from the heat because of me, while water drained from the houses of my classmates and was dumped on me by the name of my father, that summer I grew up.

Overnight I had begun to display what Sebastiano Laquidara no longer had: a body. I wore stretch shorts, cut-off flowered shirts, bras that hooked in front, canvas sneakers, fluorescent rubber bracelets. I no longer wore glasses but soft contact lenses, of a new generation; I had gone to the optometrist with my mother, who, not content to sit in the waiting room, had followed me into the doctor's office and pulled out a fan along with complaints about the early heat. He listened to her while I practiced in front of a mirror in the corner: wash your hands, soap them carefully, dry them well, place the lens on the index finger, widen the right eye with the left hand. I had gotten good at it right away, which happens in the disciplines we learn on the margins, in a solitude far from the distraction of others; as soon as that alien thing had hit the center of the iris my gaze opened up. No more blurred outlines, no dim, dirty view; but, standing up with nothing on my nose, I was afraid of losing my balance, I felt exposed. My mother had paid the doctor and saved the receipt in her wallet, satisfied that the destiny of normality she had established for me was complete.

For some time she had been pursuing only that: bury my childhood and our misfortune, open me up to summer, to the impertinent light, to sweat and an unrestrained adolescence, sweep away ugliness and affliction. And if my father had decided to miss all this, if he hadn't wanted to be present at the initiation of my life as a woman, so much the worse for him. So said every new gesture of my mother's, intended to convince me that it was worth the trouble to live and to forget, and I, with my suddenly naked eyes, after a few days had learned to put on makeup to hide small blue veins in my eye sockets that I didn't even know I had.

I took the photo out of the album, from the second page, where I'd lifted up the transparent plastic. That other Ida Laquidara stared at me from the past, laughing, and she was laughing at me; she was sixteen and I more than twice that, I would get sick and die while she would keep for herself an immovable age, like my father's, like the age of all the objects in the house. Eyes closed, I sniffed the scent of the spray that weighed down her dark curly hair, and in my legs, which had remained slender, there was still a memory of those adolescent calves. Here I am, this is me, said the pose: in it the girl challenged the lens, no longer a child and not yet adult, childhood behind her and twenty distant as a Siren. Sitting on the wall of a hotel terrace, legs dangling, feet in loafers, she was touching her hair with a charming gesture and smiling at Sara, who was taking the photo, while behind her Ortygia shone white. At school they made us learn every bit of that Greece from which Sicily was born like a rib, and we liked feeling part of it; the teachers organized our class trips according to when the tragedies were staged and the archaeological sites open, heedless of the climate, the heat, and the humidity.

"What are you looking at?" My mother entered the room, and came to sit next to me on the bed. The warmth of her arms, her hips, her legs annoyed me and I moved. "What year was that?" she asked, staring at the album.

"Can I ask you a favor?" I said. "Would you make me a coffee?"

She nodded and before going out she turned.

"Yes, but enough of that *scuntintizza*, that discontent, leave that nonsense to the radio, put it in other people's mouths."

So my mother listened to the program.

We had never talked about it, and I was surprised to imagine her in the kitchen with her hands in the sink, or lying on the couch paging through an antiques magazine, or on the telephone with one of her friends, the hum of voices in the background and the host, who, reading the stories I had written, imbued my words with tragedy or comedy. I saw clearly what she did during the broadcast, I saw her clench her teeth, tighten her fists, frown, react with her whole self to the traces I was scattering in the plots, attributing them to listeners: stories of daughters without fathers, of separated fathers, of unaffectionate or desperate mothers, stories of loss and dissatisfaction, rage and discoveries, stories of reuniting around death and mourning. Once, at the height of audience success, I had felt secure enough to have a fake Calabrian character utter my favorite proverb: "It's Christmas here on the Strait: *triulu, malanova, e scuntintizza*—complaint, bad news, and discontent." It was the story of a man alone, a widower of around sixty, who had a difficult relationship with his children. Thus I discovered from my mother's sharp remark that she listened, and not with pride in her daughter's work but, rather, to record the *scuntintizza* I poured into the imaginary stories of others—she pointed to the evidence of how wrong I was, and wouldn't forgive me. She would have liked me to show her that she had been a good mother, the best. I should have reassured her: No, I hadn't inherited from him the sadness and lack of interest in life, yes, I was outgoing and healthy, normal, like her. My mother would have liked to receive the following message from me: Don't worry, my father's disappearance isn't your fault, it's no one's fault. But unlike her I didn't think that no one was at fault: I thought we all were.

The young Ida Laquidara went on speaking to me from the photo. That summer she had kissed a boy she didn't love and felt nothing; they had lingered talking on the beach at sunset, then had walked along the shore to the steps leading to the square where he had parked his motorbike. Along the seafront were two old cannons from the Bourbon artillery, aimed at the Calabrian coast; the boy had turned and clasped her hips with his hands, as if he were following a manual, while the water reflected the last of the daylight and the inexpert Ida Laquidara thought: Sara has already done it. Just before their mouths came together she stopped, a moment, sorry—and spit the chewing gum into her hand. The boy, patient, waited for her. Then he approached again and there were no more excuses, not even a pair of glasses to shift. You ruined the magic moment for some gum, Sara had laughed when she told her, and Ida, bragging: See, I'm the wrong ingredient, the one that makes the mayonnaise curdle.

That's it, immovable girl? Is that the most you can get out of your static smile? The story of a kiss evidently late chronologically, at the outer limit of the age predicted for you; the obvious complicity between friends; the body that opens up without leaving traces in the logbook?

The girl in the photo is silent, the house is muggy and quiet. She insists on being sixteen, she wants to stay there inescapably, she doesn't even suspect that she won't be that age forever. Someone behind her, beyond the terrace, a ghost in the wind, whispers: Life is *ein Augenblick*, a blink of the eye, but it's an echo from German class, that's where she heard the word. Behind the smile, Ida Laquidara is sure she'll be like that forever. She thinks, and no one would be able to dissuade her, that everything will happen within the appearance she has now, within the precise force of a single age. Girl stopped in time, listen to me: The woman who today bears your name respects you enough not to call you a child. The sanctimonious compassion of adults is alien to the woman who's clutching the photo, so you can take a chance, give her a reward.

Courage.

Only you can stage that memory. Precisely that one.

It must have happened a week or two after returning from Ortygia: ten days after the photo and twenty after the kiss on the beach, those are the calculations if I persist in making them, but although the summers seemed very long, time was in fact patched together, insubstantial, the universe shifted in one direction and then another, every change was *ein Augen-blick*, a blink of the eye between one month and the next, long, empty weeks to colonize before the start of school.

One morning Sara telephoned me: I'm coming to pick you up in an hour, what bathing suit will you wear? Come and pick me up in what, I answered, did you buy a motor-bike last night? With Fabio, she said, we're going to the beach in Calabria, to Scylla. I hung up the telephone stunned, but not so much that I didn't enjoy the news: they would come in the car, we would take the ferry and spend a day on the opposite coast—what could be more wonderful? Outside the island the rules collapsed: outside the island one could do anything. In a two-piece bathing suit I went into my moth-er's room to look in the mirror for my new body, the slender legs, the hips just emerging, the breasts vanishing inside two small triangles of material—the body I would take into the water and along the shore. Yes, let's cross the sea and get to the other side.

Since the end of school Sara had been going out with Fabio, if going out means rounding the corner from home and getting in the car of someone who's waiting for you every day; she loved him, if love means putting your arms around his neck and opening your mouth, offering him your tongue (he's a really good kisser, she had told me proudly—and I would have liked to ask, How do you know, since you've never kissed anyone else? Or have you kissed someone else?); he loved her, if love means tickling her legs under the skirt and, defying everyone, appearing intimate with a girl who until a few days before had belonged not to him but to her parents, to school, and also to me. I put on the expression of someone who has her own things to do, so that no one would think I'd been left with the worst role, the false friend. Fabio was one of us, I repeated to myself, waiting for them in front of the house. I'd kissed the boy I didn't love at sunset on the beach with the two cannons because he was there, to be closer to my friend in my own twisted way, and it had worked. That day, though, it wouldn't, but at first I didn't realize it, dazed by my insistence on happiness, by the intoxication of crossing the Strait. *Ein Augenblick*: we spend our life blinking our eyes, and then one blink, one alone among many, changes our direction and throws what we are into disarray.

On the boat we're still together, we lean out over the parapet and sing, I say: In the sea that goes to Stromboli you can see dolphins (I think: In the boat with my father heading toward Stromboli one morning at dawn I saw holes in the water and fish tails like leaping tuna—they were dolphins). Sara says: Here at most we'll see Charybdis (I think: a sea monster who devours everything he finds, boats, men, fish, wreckage, an insatiable monster). Fabio smokes and doesn't take off his dark glasses, we drink icy beer, eat nothing, I get him to offer a cigarette and then another, I smoke awkwardly but strike a lot of poses; at the first remark implying I'm a mooch I'm embarrassed, and when we get off at Villa San Giovanni I go into a tobacco shop and spend half my money to buy three packs of cigarettes, one for each.

The beach is very white, and very crowded. Sara and Fabio are in a constant embrace, they laugh with each other, speak to each other in a vocabulary that's not mine; I pretend to understand—they can't humiliate me like that. At some point he says: I feel like a martini, and she follows him, turns and smiles at me, disappears, they disappear together. I wonder why they wanted me with them, I hate myself for falling for it and pretend it doesn't matter. I always pretend it doesn't matter, always. When it comes to that skill I'm a professional: it's three years since my father disappeared, at hiding grief I'm the best.

I get up and go toward the water.

Invincible, I go into the cold water, my bathing suit loosens, my muscles contract, I come out and return to my towel, my beer is there, planted in the sand. You can't drink it so warm, it's disgusting, says a man from a neighboring towel, pointing to my bottle. He must have sat down while I was swimming. It's the voice of a man my father's age, but I no longer know my father's voice. I take a cigarette from my purse as if I'd been smoking all my life, Fabio has the lighter, why didn't I buy three? I feel the shadow on my arm and an alien warmth, a dark arm that offers me the lighter, I hear the splutter, the flame, and the determination of a body that is sitting next to me. Did you come by yourself? No, with my friends. Nice friends to leave you alone. He's right: there are no towels, bags, things—nothing. Around me emptiness, meters of pale sand and a few rocks. I seem like a child who's telling lies. My skin feels tight from the salt.

How old are you? Eighteen. It's not true. Eighteen. Is this the first time you've come to this beach? I say I'm enrolling in the university, I'm going to study film, I'm going to live in Bologna. I lie without hesitation. I study my toenails: I should have put polish on them. He has dark curly hair and a beard, he wears eyeglasses despite the sun, and behind them are light-brown pupils. He doesn't have the smell that everyone has at the beach, he doesn't smell of sunscreen, I recognize the bath foam he washed with, I've seen the commercial, sitting at the table with my mother: at lunch, while I divide the morning from the afternoon, in the evening when she falls asleep and I sit, eyes wide on the television screen. I look past him, toward the towel, where there's a fanny pack and a hardback novel with a yellow cover from which the top of a pen sticks out instead of a bookmark. He teaches at the university, English literature.

And you? he insists. I'm going to live in Bologna, I insist on lying.

On the shore two girlfriends laugh and talk with their hands on their hips, in the water up to their knees.

He asks: Would you like another beer?

A little girl dragged to the shore by her mother screams, chafed by the sand that's getting in her flippers; one of the two friends has gone in the water while the other stands still, staring at an undefined point.

We flick the ashes into the neck of my bottle, there's warm beer in the bottom. I say: I'll finish drying off and let's go.

I play in the sand with one hand and he says nothing.

When I pull up my shorts my bathing suit is still wet, but I don't feel like staying on the beach to get hot, we cross the burning sand, we cross the street we have to cross and reach the car. I have a lot of cassettes, he says. We get in and turn on the stereo, I choose Italian music of decades before my birth, I stretch out my legs and say something wrong, seductive, everything that happens from that moment is unpleasant: sucking, kissing, detaching, the inevitable pene-tration as irksome as the two-piece bathing suit stuck to my skin. The man for whom what is happening seems inevitable now decides to linger where the skin is pale, under the marks of the bathing suit, he asks if I like it and if it's the first time I say yes and then no and both things are true: it can't be my first time, I can't let it happen like this.

If it happens to the body it hasn't really happened.

No one has passed by the car; in front of the windshield are sharp thorns and small fire-red berries, inedible.

When I leave, he also gets out. I tell him not to come with me, there's no need, I'm going to find my friends, in his satisfied eyes I read the mockery, it's clear to him that my friends don't exist, that I'm alone, and he says goodbye with an affectionate caress, asks if I want to see him again, he's sorry he doesn't have a pen to write his phone number on the palm of my hand, so he tells me, pronouncing the numbers clearly, I repeat one, two, three times, forgetting it as I recite.

I walk from the parking lot to the beach. I'm powerful, bold, I take off my clothes without even stopping, I go into the sea and swim with my head underwater and then above, freestyle, breaststroke, backstroke, then underwater again, until I hear a muffled, familiar voice. I take my head out, Sara's shouting, euphoric, from the shore, they're calling me, it's late.

I don't think about anything anymore.

On the way back we sing beside the parapet, we talk again about dolphins, we open more cold beers, we finish our packs of cigarettes; I buy mint gum and rub it on my fingers to take away the smell of smoke. The mind obliterates before you take a shower, and more completely: I'm convinced that it's so, and from then on I will repeat that fiction whenever I need it. It's a scene in present time, a dream. It's a scene I can forget in the morning.

If it happens to the body it doesn't count, if it happens to the body it didn't really happen.

"You wanted it and then you didn't drink it."

My mother pointed to the cup of coffee that had been hot and was now tepid. I hadn't realized she'd brought it to me, I hadn't even thought of it again, after asking for it, asking her to make it. I closed the album I was holding open on my lap, I said farewell to the sixteen-year-old Ida, and from the pile I took another right away.

"You're like that all day, what's the sense."

"Like what."

"You promised you'd help me."

"Sorry, I was tired when I got here. I was working on the program's summer series."

"Take a walk. A swim in the sea." She glanced contemptuously at the images of the past. "Go out, they're just photos."

"You remember when I rubbed ice on my pillow to sleep?"

"What did you do?"

"But that winter, do you at least remember that?"

I pointed to a Polaroid of her and my father under an ochre blanket, in the bed in their room. Sunday atmosphere, my mother disheveled, barely awake; she was laughing, looking in one direction, my father edging away, he was saying something, admiring her, adoring. She in a blue cotton T-shirt, he bare-chested. Under the blanket their legs were entwined, they were holding hands. I had taken the picture.

"Did you love each other?"

"Have I ever asked you anything about your husband?"

My mother's voice had turned dark and intimidating. My husband and I didn't have photos of the two of us, and she had never presumed to understand my marriage. He was shy, I considered photos of couples vulgar: two human beings who pass some time together, usually after emerging from another couple, two people who find themselves sharing some of their days, who claim to show the world a happiness that is bound to age badly, and is ousted by a new happiness that will be just as transient.

"My husband didn't get up one morning and decide to disappear."

"You don't know anything, Ida. No one knows what's in a marriage, except the husband and wife. Sometimes not even them."

"But I can talk about my father. And all the afternoons when you weren't there, and the mornings when you went out early to go to work, I was with him, even the morning he left—where were you?"

"You were a child, what do children know?"

"You left him to me every day. I don't even know if you really suffered."

"You were always like that, someone who doesn't listen, who invents other people's characters, the way you invent those stories you write for the radio. Where I was you know. At the museum, that morning as always. Your father no longer had a job: must I remind you that you ate thanks to me? Do you remember or not, that without your mother you wouldn't have had food on the table?"

"It would be better if children were brought up by the entire community, not by two parents, if they belonged to a town, a village, not to a biology. So maybe that terrible sense of property wouldn't exist."

"What are you saying? What are you saying to your mother?"

She jumped up suddenly; the high sun coming through the window focused her in a small cone of brightness, so that she resembled a ballerina on a stage, quick-tempered and light. At sixty-eight my mother was still beautiful, even more so than in the album on my lap.

"Aren't you ashamed, you should be ashamed of thoughts like that. And then you came here to do what? At least you could help me with the workers. You're here or you're not here, it doesn't change anything. I'm always alone. You ask me if I suffered?"

"I was about to go up and check the wall of the cistern, I want to see how far they've gotten."

"And what do you want to say to them about the wall? They knocked it down, if only that were the problem, Ida."

My mother's voice was a wind rising, a sandstorm preparing to strike me in the face. Could the De Salvos, on the terrace, hear her? I feared her anger as once I had feared that the unrepeatable words of our fights would reach the neighbors' ears. We were adults, I grown and she old, she couldn't start treating me like a child again, forcing me into that monstrous old game. I didn't want to be compelled to prove to myself that I would know how not to fall for it. But then would I in fact know?

"Nothing ever matters to you. You haven't changed, you're always the one who doesn't give a damn about her mother. You're the biggest egotist I know. And I gave birth to you."

I was assailed by a confusion that I didn't know how to take hold of, from which direction: I picked it up with open hands and organized a defense.

"Mamma, you know very well I came here for you."

"For me! Ever since you got here I've been waiting for a gesture, the slightest gesture. Listen to what you're saying: you came for me. As if it were a favor. You don't condescend to give your mother a glance, you don't even know what a mother is. I hope you have children one day, have a child as I had you, give that child everything as I did for you, and get nothing in return, like the nothing you give me. Why don't you have children, Ida? Are you afraid the harm you've done me will be turned against you? Are you afraid of growing up? Is it your husband? Is he the one who doesn't want children?"

I had been ingenuous enough to believe that we would be able to avoid the ferocity that had been silenced for years, but neither distance nor age had made a dent in the rage that bound us.

"What haven't you told me, Ida? You come here and you

don't even know who your mother is, there you are in Rome writing your fantasy stories, with a husband who doesn't deign to appear, I have to inform you that the ceiling is falling down here, and all day you're looking at the past like an idiot. I have an idea you live like that, letting life go by as if it weren't yours."

The sandstorm blew through the holes. Spirals of wind whirled grains upon grains, they whipped my arms and calves.

"I would like to know who put it into your head to behave like this. Nothing, you will leave nothing after you, you sow nothing. I didn't bring you up like that. My conscience is in order, I did my duty as a mother even by myself, even without your father: school, university, you lacked nothing, a mother's love, you have your home. Why don't you have children, Ida? Because you want to impress on me that what happened to us ruined our existence? If I managed to forget it, why shouldn't you, who were a child? Why don't you talk to me? If my mother were alive I would go down on my knees and kiss her hands."

At that moment I understood what a mother really is: something from which there is no protection. It's said that a mother gives everything and asks nothing; no one says that she asks everything and gives what we don't ask to have.

In the years since my father's disappearance, my mother had massed her personal storm: sometimes she would display it, sometimes not, sometimes she would let it out and at others shut it up. I was the object of her rage but not the cause, so my attempts to diminish it would always be insufficient. I would be able to defend myself from her with all my tricks and my experience, I could try to force her to stop and maybe I would succeed, but every stratagem would evaporate and we would finally be alone, facing one another. My failures would shatter against the walls. Why didn't I have children? I didn't know, I knew only that neither my husband nor I could accept the idea of bringing into the world a creature who might die before us, causing us intolerable pain and regret, or who would die after us but inexorably, thus making those who had borne him guilty. That's what it seemed to me: a load of suffering without end and without a light, and if this meant that I had inherited from my father the tendency to be depressed, then so be it.

I should have answered my mother with what I knew.

I don't want children because I'm afraid they'll die, they'll disappear, because I'm afraid that love will disintegrate between Pietro and me, I don't have children because they didn't come and we never went looking for them. I don't have children because I don't want a human being to be born inside me and live in me at its pleasure. I don't have children because they pass through the body, the place I can control, even convince myself that if it happened to the body it didn't really happen.

"I don't have children because Pietro and I sleep at night. We're not together. As a couple, I mean."

The storm stopped.

"What is it, Mamma? Do I have to explain it to you? Now that I have the words they frighten you; we don't make love anymore, we don't use the bed for that. We sleep like the two of you in the last months, when Papa didn't get up, and you said: Look what your father does in our bed, look what the bed has become. As if the bed were the problem, and not the suffering. You said: It doesn't work anymore, as if it were an object, a kitchen utensil. You repeated it to me how many times, three, four, to make sure I understood that it was he who wasn't doing his duty, not you, you must have told me that you, unlike him, were fine, a good wife, even if you forgot to clean the toothpaste off the sink. I, too, would have run away from a wife like that, who humiliated me in front of my daughter."

"I never said it in front of him."

"Only because we were in another room, separated by the hall? The walls in this house are made of butter. You know what I say to you? Sell it. You want to give it away? What do I care. It's full of unhappiness, this place."

When my mother left the room the luminous cone in which she'd moved remained empty, and I drank a cup of spoiled coffee.

Fourth Nocturne (Afternoon)

I sleep on my stomach, head crushing the left cheek, a circle of saliva on the pillow. Pietro arrives, he doesn't speak, he's in a good mood. He stops next to the bed, as if to watch over me, a sly light in his eyes.

My husband has a quality that explodes when I'm half asleep: with him you're comfortable, really comfortable. His presence always brings something warm, invisible, and essential. That Pietro is indispensable I realize when he's not there, I can tell from how much I miss him, from the disquiet I feel with others; in his absence I learn to love his presence. Without him the uneasiness I feel among people is exaggerated. If he died I'd want to die, too, and certainly I would die of solitude.

In sleep there's Pietro, and with him events and people are less frightening to me.

The Things We Don't Do

As soon as I woke up I thought again of the last exchange—I couldn't call it a conversation—with my mother. I would have said I'm sorry, I didn't mean to offend you, I would have apologized, taking a step back: I didn't want to destroy the cardboard crèche she had struggled to erect over the years, calling it family without distinguishing between affection and biology, between fate and choice. I thought of my father, depressed and a slave to drugs, with no more sexual desire; I thought of my mother, a woman who, still young, had endured the negation of her body, suffered the irreversibility of spent drives. In the mirror of their marriage I saw mine and all the marriages of the world run aground, imprisoned in the claim of having beside us a unique person whom we've asked to be lover, companion, family, friend, only to witness, devastated, the inevitable collapse of one of these definitions or all of them together. I at least had had the courage to remove one bar from the cage: my husband wouldn't be a father, not of my children. And yet not even that had saved our marriage from turning into a lame creature.

With my father still present but now incapable of playing a role, my mother must have floundered in the cage: she could no longer be a wife, being a mother in the abstract didn't interest her, whereas being my mother did, because she possessed the capacity to desire nothing but her own fate, and this I called conservation, and feared above all else. So it had happened that she loved me and only me, and that love wounded me rather than taking care of me. In her way she had accepted the silence I imposed on her, in return for the silence she had imposed on me: concerning our marriages a prudent and mutual code of silence was in force. For a long time she had walked on the edge without asking, and I had grown used to not getting questions about the children I didn't have, about my work, about my man; in the early years, when I returned to Messina for the holidays, always in a hurry and for the few necessary nights, I would put my suitcase down on the floor and end up not wearing the clothes I had brought from Rome. I opened the closet and pulled out shapeless sweaters, plain colored socks, blue pajamas, shawls, tight shiny skirts; I chose what I could wear and put the rest back. Five drawers were full of children's clothes, a small striped waterproof coverall, the bottle warmer, leather children's shoes, a sea-green plastic die with two loud bells inside—things saved so that one day I could dress and entertain my children. Those things had become funny and immediately old, then sad and finally useless; soon they would be grotesque. In the first drawer my mother had also saved photos of

us as adults, letters, documents, yellowed clippings from
the local newspaper: the two scholarships I'd won in high
school, the obituaries of my grandparents, the short article
on my father's disappearance. Birth, death, disappearance,
all in the same drawer, the pacifier and mourning, childhood and old age, school and my merits, and then the day
without time that had split our life, a few lines on the disappearance of Sebastiano Laquidara, esteemed high school
teacher, for me the proof that it had really happened, the
evidence that that was the way things had gone: a man, a
body, had been my father, and then had disappeared. And
your children, you won't bring me any? My mother didn't
ask then, and I wasn't compelled to answer.

Outside of here, in the new city, the things we didn't do
held my husband and me together: we didn't have a child,
we didn't buy an apartment, we didn't plan a trip to the other
side of the world. We'll go next year, we said of the journey;
as for the apartments we visited with the agents, they were
never our size, one too small, another didn't have balconies,
another would have forced us to change neighborhoods,
whereas renting is convenient, renting doesn't tie us down,
we said, winding like climbing plants around the house we
didn't buy. We built castles in the air only to knock them
down into a useless drift. Children didn't come, and neither
of us talked about looking for them, going to get them, I was
used to absences and my husband got used to them with me;
we would grow old beside each other, we would grow old
under the gaze of our contemporaries who became parents
and parents again, still reproducing at the age our father and
mother were when as children we looked at them, the age

of ochre-colored blankets, the age when Mamma and Papa were adults but still young and fertile. I had fixed my parents at that age forever, an age clear in memory, an age that my husband and I were about to reach and pass.

Now my mother had demanded to enter into my marriage, to know what happened between Pietro and me. I hadn't been able to prevent her, and so I had also entered into hers.

I decided to join her; she must have gone to the place where the aspect of the house was changing—above our heads. But she wasn't on the roof. In her stead was a hood formed of heat and clouds, a roof over the roof, the air excited and wild, saturated with dampness, and Nikos by himself, lying on the floor with his arms folded, while the wind shook the television antennas and cables.

He rose onto his elbows. "Your mother went back down."

Was it possible that I hadn't seen her? I was alarmed, maybe she was in the kitchen, why hadn't she heard me go out? Maybe she didn't feel like talking to me, after the fight. Another more definite and angrier thought pushed that one out: Nikos was making himself master of my terrace, comfortable and peaceful as if it were his, but it was mine, I repeated again: mine. I couldn't take my eyes off his scar. I squatted down next to him, so that I, too, was on the floor. The sky thundered, I wound my fingers around my legs pulled up to my chest, Nikos stared at my hands.

I felt then a possible intimacy and was tempted to tell him about the red box. There's a reason I came here, I would say, and I'm the only one who knows it, I haven't yet told anyone: not even myself. You see my fingers, I would insist, lowering my gaze to follow his: What's in the box I put there with these hands.

"My left hand," I began instead, "did you see my left hand?" I extended the arm and spread the fingers. "It's no good, I had a problem when I was born, see?" I squeezed together the pinkie and the ring finger. "They were attached when I was born, I had to have an operation as a child, I had palms like a duck's."

"How old were you?"

"Eight," I replied seriously. "It was very sad, especially before—my classmates made fun of me."

Nikos didn't answer right away, the air darkened.

"I'm sorry," he said finally.

I shrugged. Two hornets buzzed around us, uncertain whether to chase each other or fight. I started laughing. "It's nonsense, it's not true, nothing's true."

"Then why'd you say it?"

"No reason. I told that once to a boyfriend, he was worried, embarrassed, he didn't know what to do."

"Then you told him the truth?"

"Right away. I wanted to seem interesting, we were twenty. At your age you experiment, try things out, whereas I didn't do anything."

"It was better then, not like now." Nikos showed no doubts. No one knows how to be reactionary and old-fogeyish like a twenty-year-old, only certain proud, wayward kids seek that type of comfort in the myth of values, condemning the disastrous corruption of the present.

"Why, how is it now, do you think?"

"There's too much freedom, it was better before when things were clearer and you couldn't do what you wanted."

"Apart from the fact that I'm not two hundred years old, look, the era you're talking about never existed: everyone has always done everything, secretly or in front of others."

I hadn't convinced him.

"Before, women would choose a man and keep him for a lifetime."

"Did your mother do that?"

"Like all women."

"She's from Crete, right?"

He nodded.

"Do you like it? Do you all ever go back there?"

"Of course, have you been?"

I kept the memory for myself. I had been there with my husband the summer after we were married; neither of us had felt like calling it a honeymoon, but early one morning it had been precisely that. The colors of dawn lingered without fading, we had bought a *bougatsa* just out of the oven and had gone to eat it up at the fortress on the peninsula of Paleochora, the sea on the sides and us in the middle. We had sat close together for a long time, suspended and raised up over the rest, a perspective not so different from what Nikos and I had on the roof.

"Yes, I've been there. Anyway Sicily is Greek land, your mother's happy here, isn't she?"

"She's unhappy."

"Does she have other children?"

"I have a sister who's seventeen. Are you happy?"

"No one is."

A louder thunderclap arrived, this time more than a warning, and I turned toward the cistern next to us: every night in summer when, after sunset, the city closed the aqueduct, that supply came to the aid of my mother and me. The autoclave was the divinity of our earth, silent and favorable over our heads. Thanks to it we had never suffered drought.

"How's it going with my mother?"

"She's nice, she checks everything."

"She's demanding with her family's house."

"It's your house, too."

"I live in Rome."

"Each of us has only one house, in life. My mother in her mind lives in Chania, the city where she was born."

It was one of the places I'd loved most on Crete. I remembered the Venetian profile of the harbor and two glasses of *raki* my husband and I had drunk at sunset.

It started raining.

The first drops fell, thickened, and caught us while we stood up and decided to run, before I could guess how to answer Nikos, what chinks to open for him, what to show him of my existence outside the house. But I liked the rain, I slowed down purposely so I would get wet, not be spared invasion to the farthest corners of material and skin, until the storm really shook the sky. Nikos sheltered in the empty shed, while I gave a last glance at the wild flashes of lightning on the leaden horizon, wrung out the wet ends of my hair and fled down the stairs.

Entering, I found my mother near the door.

She was wearing a long short-sleeved cotton bathrobe with small patches of embroidery, and she was sitting on a blue velvet stool no one ever sat on: a stool at the front door isn't for sitting on but for putting down coats, bags, rain-soaked purses when you've just come in from outside, and we had always used it like that. Once my father, complaining about the oddities of the house—"the ugliest I've ever lived in"—had enumerated the ridiculous objects, leaving out the boards of his bookshelf, the only piece of furniture that for him was untouchable, cloaked in useful objects, books. The most unpresentable of all for him was the stool. Have you ever seen a stool at the door? he had asked, speaking more to himself than to me, and I had giggled, to confirm that I was on his side. My father didn't look for my complicity, but I was quick to supply it, in order not to damage even a moment of our afternoons. I winked to let him know that I was on his side, that life began when, once my homework was finished and his beanpoles disposed of, he and I could go by ourselves to the *passeggiatammare* to train together for my imminent competitions. I hadn't told him that, waiting for him to come out of the bathroom, I leaned on the stool to lace up my skates. I had kept to myself its usefulness, but starting the next day I laced up the skates in my room, sitting on the bed or the floor.

"I got ground meat for dinner," my mother said. "I made it in white sauce, I remember you like it that way, in the bain-marie."

Her voice was gentle and sad, and I had no desire to torture her again with the past.

Fifth Nocturne

Before going to sleep I call my husband. The telephone rings in vain, and someone else might worry, but not me, I know everything about him, he's never betrayed me, and then betrayal is nothing, half sentences and an excess of truths have already broken in two what we are, we loved each other and wounded each other and slept beside each other separate and wild, we showed ourselves vulnerable and incompatible, irrevocably, and discovered every time that you don't die of the irrevocable. We've been married for ten years, we'd known each other for eight months when I asked him, Marry me, I've never wanted anything in life, it's the first time I've wanted something with all my might, that's what I said to him. Eight months was even too long, I already knew what he would offer: refuge for me, refuge and remedy for what I was, I wanted only that, I'd wanted it forever. But now I'm calling him and my husband doesn't answer, the things we haven't said assail me, knock at the windows. It's stopped raining, it's midnight, and my husband is sleeping. I push the telephone far away from the bed.

I think of my father's body and last night's dream, tonight my mother brought meat and vegetables to the table, just as she did twenty-three years ago, as if I had to wake up tomorrow and go to school, as if the black-and-fuchsia backpack at the foot of the bed under a hill of biology, literature, Latin books had never been put down, as if the objects scattered in the room still occupied the place they occupied. If I don't sleep I have to protect myself from the girl on the beach at Scylla, who enjoys tormenting me. My body is hers, I summon vertebrae, nails, hair, joints, but to no avail, I feel nothing.

With one hand I pick up the telephone, the silent luminous screen says: three missed calls.

"Good night," my husband has finally written, and then: "I love you."

Tomorrow he'll want to talk to me, and I don't want the voices of others, not even his, I already regret having tried to call him; I'll think up something, it's not right to speak, not yet, not now. I'm in bed, I'm extremely tired, finally I fall asleep and I dream.

My mother is laughing, lying down, turned on one side toward me, disheveled and happy as in the photo, I intuit the ochre-colored blanket in a tangle at her feet. She has just hugged me, she looks at me gratefully, she doesn't have the smile proper for a daughter, my mother isn't laughing at me, she hasn't hugged me, my body isn't me: in the dream I'm the body of my father.

Terrible Things as if They Were Normal, and Perhaps the Reverse

The damage, I reflected in the morning under the cold water of the shower—the increasing damage was contained in me in the form of good manners. While others reacted to suffering by becoming aggressive, for me it was better to hide aggression. The last trace of my father was hidden with cruel tenacity in an unflappable and proverbial cordiality much loved by strangers: the more remote they were, the more they loved it; the less they knew of me, the more they praised my courtesy, especially if they'd met me through my husband—his colleagues, his few friends, his modest relatives. Politeness protected me.

The appearance of meekness I had upon arriving in Rome came from Sicily, I had watered and cared for my politeness in adolescence, when my mother and I wanted the world to stay away from us, as far away as possible, and we had understood that the simplest way to keep people away was to be very courteous toward them. By ourselves, within our walls, we succumbed to the house and the absence that pervaded it, but on the street, in the supermarkets, at school and at work, at the movies, in the shops, on the landing, at the windows of banks and post offices, we smiled often. We didn't show wounds or appear defenseless, we didn't ask for help; people were considerate about the void that had marked our existence and we repaid them by praising their full lives, to each we said the nice thing, and if someone insisted on looking for conflict we turned our backs and let him howl at the moon, incensed and incredulous, isolated, reluctant to accept being nothing in the face of our secret war. We didn't fight with others, we didn't have time. They passed before us: those who wished to cheat us on the change at the cash register, those who overtook us when we were slow to start up at the traffic signal, those who raised the neighboring terrace three centimeters higher than ours. And, before that damage was transmuted into dampness in our walls, even the evangelicals were unimportant. But the danger of others' happiness was always lying in wait, could offend us continuously, we could never stop protecting ourselves: our cordiality guarded the wound like a sniper, defending with its weapons the border between us and the world. When, on the other hand, we were safe, my mother and I unceasingly covered up, and covering up we atoned; we had failed, but no one knew it, we were guilty, a depressed man had turned away from life because we hadn't been able to hold on to him, we thought our guilt was a scarlet stain and unpunished.

Two years after my father's disappearance, we were at the beach, and a woman began calling her son: Sebastiano,

Sebastiano. My mother and I, on our separate mats, stared at the water. That name wounded me, I prayed that the child would come out of the sea and the voice would stop calling him, that he would return to shore, I prayed that he would obey and she would not utter that name again, Sebastiano, Sebastiano—that was all you could hear in the whole bay, Sebastiano. My mother remained mute behind her sunglasses. It was our punishment: a name that we no longer uttered, repeated to wound our ears. The unconsciousness of others was our enemy, the dailiness of others was our enemy, the names of others were our enemies.

In the years of his depression, my father had lost more and more of his friends, until he didn't have any. He and my mother, both orphaned, had enclosed themselves in a sticky cocoon, and my father's illness had done the rest; the days following his disappearance had been days of fruitless searching and questioning, was it really possible that no one had seen him, no shopkeeper, no fisherman along the shore? In those days only one of my father's few acquaintances who had visited the house turned out to be useful to me: not because he had news or because he could really bring me any comfort but because he suggested what would become my truth. We were in the living room, a room usually closed, my mother had removed the sheets that normally covered the couches, and this man—white beard and hair, kind eyes, chubby hands—whom I had seen sometimes next to my father in the class photos from the Juvarra school, had asked if I liked to swim. I nodded. Like your father, he responded. I was thirteen, an age when one believes only in details. I had gone to sleep devastated and confused by the mourning without a corpse that shadowed our house, but I couldn't stop thinking about that man's words: my father liked the sea. I remembered long summers spent swimming together, and I remembered the day that routine ended, because of a terrible fear in my mother's gaze when my father, already depressed and thinner, didn't emerge from a long swim. How did that man know that my father loved to swim, had he told him, had they gone to the beach together? My mother had introduced me, he was the principal of the Juvarra school, then why, if he seemed so kind, had he agreed that my father should leave his job? Pondering, I learned two things: that people don't have a single face, and that my father must, of necessity, have returned to the water.

In the days that followed I began to be resigned. If my father had chosen the sea, that was the element through which he would speak to us, and it hardly mattered that the search recovered no trace of his remains, that on no beach had he been seen alive. From that moment on, I would listen to the water.

You went through terrible things as if they were normal, and perhaps the reverse, Pietro had said to me once. He knew about me without ever having asked, in the only way we need to know the facts of those we love, because we know them, period.

Other People's Houses

"So weren't you supposed to go and talk to the neighbors?"

My mother was right, I had promised. I had to deal with the floor and those three arrogant centimeters; I had put it off and there had been the storm, but the sun was shining again.

Standing in front of the closet, I chose a light dress in autumnal colors that had belonged to my mother. The background was ochre, like the blanket that enveloped her in the photo with my father, and it had a pattern of intertwined leaves and a mandarin collar fastened by two white buttons. I buttoned them, in spite of the heat. Since I returned I hadn't worn any of the clothes I'd brought from Rome: just as in past years the suitcase sat on the floor half open and entirely full, nothing it held would be useful to me, in none of the beloved everyday clothes of the other life—mine, I said to myself insistently—would I feel comfortable. I crossed the hall and went into the bedroom to see myself in the only full-length mirror in the house; my mother was shorter than me, the dress that grazed her knees pulled up on my hips, I loosened my hair, stole a comb from the night table to hold it in place and a silver bracelet with an enameled clasp, pinched my cheeks so that I'd look less pale, and, finally, accoutered like a knight, I slipped out onto the landing.

After I rang, there were sounds of plates and children's voices, quick, cautious steps and a pause behind the door; it was opened by a woman with long brown hair held back by a hair band, wearing shorts, sandals, and a dark cotton tank top, a young mother. I recognized the third of the five children of the evangelicals; so the apartment had gone to her, hers the pile of problems, the holes in the plaster, the crumbling outside walls, the partitions to knock down and the load-bearing walls to circumvent, the choice of furniture and new objects to shelter, hers the refloorings and repaintings, the avalanche of memories and innovations, hers a world parallel to mine, in fact worse: she also had to endure the weight of fights with her siblings, of the division among equals. I, an only child, was spared at least that burden.

"Ida?!"

"You remember me?"

"I hear you on the radio."

"Oh, the texts, not the voice."

"It's my husband's favorite show."

"Thank you, really. I'm sorry, I didn't realize the time, you were probably having lunch."

"How are you? Did you just get here from Rome?"

"More or less," I explained, as if not having called her before had been a failure on my part and not the norm between two people who had never been friends but happened to share a landing. I followed as she led the way into her house.

She had eliminated the hall, an old-fashioned space, considered useless by the majority of our contemporaries, and we entered a big room: the husband and children sitting at the table, the television on, the window open to let in the air, on the high chair a colored plastic book for infants, the kind that make cries and sounds when you put your fingers on the buttons. The little girl pressed, her brother complained about the noise, the father intervened to quiet them; on the plates was pasta in tomato sauce with eggplant and basil on the side—children don't want intrusions on simple flavors.

"Carlo, look who it is, let me introduce Ida Laquidara, she came just now from Rome."

A solid young man with dark eyes and thinning hair clipped short got up to offer me his hand, a born father.

"Congratulations, I always listen to you. Eat with us, we've just begun." They said something about the children, introducing them by their names, they poured sparkling water in a glass and put a serving of pasta on another plate. I wasn't good at refusing; I hadn't said a word and already I was avoiding an excess of eggplant: "Thank you, that's fine," I resigned myself. I slid onto the chair and began to wonder about the name of the girl whose face I had met on the landing, in the doorway, whose voice I had heard dozens of times, on summer and winter evenings, when with the rest of the family she sang hymns and songs of praise to a god neither my mother nor I was concerned with because we didn't have time for him, because that god couldn't help us any more than we could help ourselves. It would have been good and useful now to start the conversation calling her by name, Marta or Stefania, a detail that would itself be the bearer of friendship, meaning: Of course, I remember, too, I've always remembered you.

"So it was here that you sang," I said instead.

She looked at me in surprise.

"At night you prayed, with your parents. In this room. This wall"—I pointed to the wall—"is shared with our living room."

"It was the living room, the kitchen was over there, I changed a few things when I got married. Did we bother you? My parents wanted to invite you, we rang the doorbell once, but you weren't there, I said: Surely they're busy . . ."

"It seems like yesterday, doesn't it?"

My question was banal, my question was false. It didn't seem like yesterday or today; rather, it was the era that I hadn't forgotten, whereas one who becomes an adult justly forgets. It wasn't yesterday or today, it was forever: even though the roof of my house was collapsing, and the walls of the house next door had been knocked down and new ones put up, even though the evangelical family had experienced its natural diaspora and beside me sat a survivor who had saved herself in whatever way she could, as I had tried to do and as everyone tries to do. I envied her the dailiness of the stove, the smell of cleanliness, the future she had gone to meet, the tablecloth that had drawings of American desserts on it and recipes in English, maybe bought on a honeymoon—there must be photos of it on the walls and in an album or on a computer, posted on the Internet, sent in a chat. And in that life that was the opposite of mine I found a life the same as mine.

"My mother," I started off at a distance. "Years ago my mother noticed that your father must have done—by himself, I imagine, because your father is the type to do these things by himself—he must have raised the floor up there, on the terrace, by five centimeters. By the way, how is he?"

In the normal world fathers grew old, they got sick, they died. Outside my house, fathers were not frightening entities made of nothing.

"He broke his wrist last week, falling in the bath—luckily my mother was with him. They moved closer to the center."

"I'm sorry."

"It's true, we did some work on the terrace, but that business of the centimeters I don't remember. My mother didn't like the color of the old tiles, she chose the new ones with my sister, how long has it been? Twenty years? We were all still here."

"It wasn't five but three, the centimeters. My mother always exaggerates."

"Giuliana, your father must have put down a new floor, as Ida says, he does things his own way, doesn't listen to anyone, plus he always makes a mess of these jobs, remember what shape we found the bathroom in."

The husband's intervention came to my aid. Giuliana. The bathroom. Proper names, common names, dialogues, floors, mistakes, small real facts, footholds.

"For years we've had problems with dampness, there are cracks in the ceiling, the paint started flaking, then the plaster. Last month there was another collapse and my mother decided to redo the roof."

"Oh Lord, Ida, I'm so sorry, I saw the workers, but why

didn't you tell us? We could have figured out a solution together. Look, my father always causes disasters . . ."

The boy threw his fork on the floor, whining in a loud voice; there was a commercial on the TV. I looked down, staring at the leaf pattern on the hem of my mother's dress, which recalled the neck that I couldn't see; my eyes were burning, my ears stinging. I wanted to cry. It would have been simple, authentic, and natural. Why hadn't we told them, what had kept us from ringing the bell and explaining? What could I say now to Giuliana, that we had ruined our life because we didn't know how to say the word "remedy"? That we were paralyzed by my father, who returned, furious, to visit us through the water that the obsessive disfigurement of those centimeters had poured insistently, more and more insistently, onto our ceiling?

What was true was the confused rattle of a child, the child I had been and was still, who had passed through a body that was adolescent and then adult. Or I should have said: I'm sorry, Giuliana, but my mother and I were absorbed in protecting ourselves; from what, she would have asked; from you, I would have had to answer, and she rightly wouldn't have understood.

"Now we have to put in a new floor, and the contractor asked us to agree on the height of the floor: we can't stay lower, but I don't want to be higher than you and cause you damage, I want the levels to be the same, but we have to specify, be sure that later, I don't know—tomorrow for some reason or other—you won't raise the floor again."

Giuliana and her husband smiled, my words had set off in both the same conspiratorial, shared thought.

"We've given the apartment to an agency to sell, my husband has been transferred to Palermo."

"It's not the moment to commute," he added, and I thought he was talking about school and the children's routines, until finally I observed my neighbor, the shirt pulled over the protruding stomach, five months, or maybe six, that secure and trusting gaze was pregnancy, the serenity of one who has nothing to lose, because she's playing at a different table.

"But of course, yes, congratulations." I hurried to camouflage my distraction, or, rather, my repression. I reread the whole dialogue in a different key, I began to cover my failure with compliments, questions, when will it be born, is it a boy or a girl, what do the other children say, there wasn't even the time for me to hear an answer before, immediately, the next question was ready. Meanwhile I picked up two rigatoni from the plate, a mouthful of eggplant, another piece of pasta. The tomato was barely cooked, the way children like it, and had the fragrance of basil even though there was no trace of leaves: most children avoid green in food, children have a chromatic appetite, greens disturb the red, the taste has to be homogeneous, sugary, compact. It wasn't a pasta for adults but a pasta cooked for the children. It was a dish thought up for them in the supermarket, like the plastic spoon with a yellow bear drawn on it, the calendar decorated with cartoon characters, and scribbles next to the dates: first day of nursery school, checkup at pediatrician, orthodontist, the baby tooth is replaced, the chicken pox comes and goes. It was the life of people who weren't afraid of transformation: children who become adults who become parents, couples who become families, desires that become writing on a calendar and walls repainted in inoffensive colors, pale but not neutral, because the passing of the years is never neutral, the generations rest on choices that aren't choices, one child then another, one house then another, the dislocated wrist of a parent who's getting old, you welcome an old acquaintance, show off a living room, move to another city, taking with you something that isn't only yourself.

Finally free of the demands of the children, who were distracted by the cartoon credits, and of the tension that had preceded the explanation for my visit, Giuliana's husband asked about my work. He loved the program I wrote for, he loved the people's stories, and we always chose stories he could identify with, he said. He asked me if they were all really true and I said yes, silencing a certain uneasiness. He added that he had written to us, sending in episodes from his life, but we had never chosen them, and he went on recounting his experiences, in detail. I couldn't concentrate, but I laughed when I had to laugh and nodded understandingly when I felt that my concern would be useful to him. I encouraged him to write again to the editors, I wasn't the one involved in choosing the proposals, I said, but I would put in a good word. Then I noted that it was late, and my mother was expecting me; I thanked them for their kindness (what kindness? I gave the eggplant all the credit). Once I got up I realized that, sitting down, pressing with hips and thighs, I had stretched out the dress: it was no longer tight. Giuliana went with me to the door and said goodbye with a hug, her stomach protruding against my mother's dress. On the landing, as I turned the key in the lock, I noticed a spiderweb neglected in the branches of a fake plant under the light switch.

In the kitchen another lunch had been prepared for me and was waiting: breaded cutlets. The bread crumbs mixed with tiny bits of garlic, cheese, and parsley covered wide tender slices. My mother had added cut-up potatoes sautéed in a frying pan: when I was a child she made them like that for frittata, but before putting them in the beaten eggs she saved some pieces for me on a secret plate in the oven, protected by a napkin, I took it out and ate them all, then I licked my fingers, greasy with oil and salt.

"No problem," I reported. "The De Salvos can raise our floor, they won't raise theirs again and will tell the next owners not to repeat the mistake."

"What? They're selling?"

"They're going to live in Palermo. You didn't tell me that Giuliana was pregnant again."

We hadn't talked about her or our neighbors, and in none of our phone calls had there ever been an opening for news of the evangelicals. My mother looked past the halo of a stain on the blind, speared two potatoes and a piece of meat and smeared the forkful in the oil, pursed her lips in the vexed expression she had whenever something unexpected inserted itself between her and the things she had chosen to ignore, concentrated on that intrusion, and we both chewed it away.

Two Black Plastic Bags

After lunch I shut myself in my room with two bags full of stuff that my mother had piled up in the study because I was supposed to consider it first: what to keep, what to throw away, what was important and what wasn't—what to get rid of and what moved us. She couldn't know that I was interested in saving only the contents of a red box at the bottom of a drawer, and yet I was curious to see what objects she had set aside for me.

I sat on the bed and began.

I thought I'd find in those bags the beating heart of her request, a scale of recollections and priorities, the sign of our shared memory, a hand reaching to draw me out of the silence of the years. Eagerly I began to rummage, remove, drop on the floor what didn't interest me: spare parts for a bicycle, unused cartridges for a printer thrown away before I moved.

That's it?

The more I rummaged, the greater my disappointment,

and dismay: my mother had assembled the objects that in her view would be useful to me, not those she imagined contained a memory. Her choice had nothing to do with memory, only with usefulness. The objects were all fairly new, brought into the house after my father's disappearance, going back to the period of his vengeful reappearance in the form of water and the following years; they were contemporary things, empty and already shriveled, they were dusty, ugly things, above all ugly. In the bags considered important by my mother there was no trace of the time when we were three, there was no memory of when that number meant me, my father, my mother. That was the original triangle, but life, for her, started from another epoch, from another number three: me, my mother, the house. And that triangle broke up, too, because the relations between us functioned like an obsessive dyad, a constant duel: my father and me, my mother and me, the house and me, mother and father. And now, in the bags on account of which she had summoned me to return immediately to what she insisted on calling our house, my mother had accumulated an undifferentiated jumble of things, united by a presumption of usefulness.

She might be able to use that, she had thought about each of those pieces of junk. She had continued to save objects that would mold a future, mine; she had stopped with the ones that were no longer useful (baby clothes, trousseau), to start again with new bits of junk that in her view were suitable for my new life and that husband she barely knew, for the new city I hadn't moved away from, for choices she felt she wanted to make less sad and precarious.

Last, I pulled out a blue metal stapler and a pen with a

crowd of butterflies drawn on it, and then I stretched my feet out on the mattress, exhausted. My dirty heels made two black spots on the white sheet.

A familiar pain arrived from far away, not the greedy languor of melancholy that needs to be fed but the clear cry of sadness that asks simply to surrender, a Siren I gave in to helplessly. From the bags rose the same unstoppable force I had found in my father's eyes, in the passivity with which he endured our false joy when we pretended that he might get better, fearing that the depression would emerge from his gaze and brush against us, like an infection. If it was an epidemic, then my father was the plague-spreader, and we couldn't protect ourselves. On an ordinary summer evening, the trauma over and winter gone—the mosquitoes tormenting our legs, the undercooked fillet on the platter, the hum of the neon and the dust on the plastic of the light fixture, the television on, with the worst summer songs—my mother and I should simply have put down our forks and said to each other: He's gone. Not talked about the dampness, not discussed the centimeters raised by the neighbors, not scratched our hands on the ice in the freezer getting out the meat, not burned our palms or forearms when we turned it on the grill, not wounded our bodies just to silence the words. Rather: we should have mixed our tears with the oil and fat of the meat, named the body of my father, created a tomb made of sentences and even tears, if necessary.

We hadn't done it, and his coffin remained everywhere.

Supine, the bags at my feet, my hands grimed by the sweaty patina of time, I struggled toward the porthole through which I could get out, take off toward the water or the light, free myself, not keep spinning in circles. But none of my thoughts moved aside to make room for my mother: you can't subject a ceremony to a transformation, a ceremony is handed down inviolable from year to year, from day to day. As always I should have acted by myself. I stretched out my arms, spread my palms, and resigned myself. Then that perfect actor who had been my father came onstage: darkness, light, a bell, the alarm clock, no more alarm clock, three numbers: six one six. My father stretched, got up, opened the closet, chose the shirt, stared at the image of himself in the mirror, chose the tie, left the wrong one on the chair, tied his shoes, looked back, and so away, out of the room, out the door, down the stairway. Curtain.

Sitting in the first row in my theater, I had ordered that scene to repeat itself a million times: not just an obsession but a compulsory ritual, the way hand-washing is for some people, or not passing between lampposts before an appointment, or dividing the objects in a room by shape and color. Rituals, only rituals: they allow us to get through a dark and threatening time by promising safety after the repetition. To each his own: mine was my father's departure from the house. Safe inside my narcotic, I could find the truth I preferred, always the same: his was a rebellion, not a surrender. My father had reacted to the fear of death and the depressive illness by cutting off my mother, me, work, the ochre-colored blanket, shirts, jackets, pots, alarm clocks, beetles, a dangerous roof, photographs that no longer resembled him, a long hall like a gallery, all those books, all that life. To death, which had checkmated him and nailed him to the bed, he had uttered the magic formula: Nothing belongs to me anymore.

Sixth Nocturne (Afternoon)

My mother and Sara and I are hiding in the bathrooms of a ship, we ended up there by mistake, or by chance, without tickets, jumping through a hatch; the hold is empty, we divide up the toilets, Sara and I in the women's, my mother in the men's. We hear voices, footsteps, they're looking for us, they discover us. Dragged out, Sara defends herself by displaying a big black bag: we found it, she swears, it wasn't us. She's right, it wasn't us, but I know that we should have kept it hidden, not talked about it with anyone, discarded it before we got on the ship. My mother brushes her hair: it's late, she says, and then we were barefoot, she adds, as if it were a sin to go around without shoes. The sailors stand in a circle around the bag and empty it cautiously, as if it contained a bomb; they pull out two legs, a wig, an arm, a stump, I don't know who that woman is, it wasn't us who tore her to pieces or stuck her in there, they'll think it was us but it wasn't, the men are angry, they shout and threaten us. The bed rejects me, the bed hates me, I wake up, the bags are still there.

Leaking

My mother wasn't sleeping. I went in to her, I sat on the chair next to the bed and spoke first.

I didn't say: It's the same bedroom where you slept with my father.

I said instead: "The film we saw that night, where a little girl goes to stay for two weeks with her grandmother, whom she's never met, you remember it?"

My mother shifted the sheet. "The one with that blond goggle-eyed American actress?"

I didn't say: There was the scene with the tree.

My mother drank some water from the night table. "I remember, it was a good movie."

It was a March evening, the second year after my father disappeared. I had the remote and was flipping through the channels seeking refuge from the news and its commentators, when I stopped on Channel 4. A little girl had arrived at her grandmother's house in the country. She was sad because her parents were going on a long trip and wouldn't take her with them; she lived in the city and barely knew the woman with blond braids and the expression of a witch. Little by little the girl is sucked into the world of jams, cupboards, goat's milk, and nighttime screech owls. At that point in the story my mother had awakened from after-dinner dozing, pulled the blanket up over her knees, and we watched together, in the dark, an innocent film. As the day of departure approached, grandmother and granddaughter decided to plant a tree that would grow, together with their bond, summer after summer.

The camera had framed the chosen rectangle of a field, their emotion-filled faces, and then the earth again. The two shovels were lowered one after the other to dig the hole. The grandmother's shovel. Clods upturned. The granddaughter's shovel. New clods.

Incapable of changing the channel, I had waited for my mother to say something first. In the silence her eyes reflected the scene, the shade of green, the brown, the gray of the shovel. My father's body couldn't be found anywhere and I couldn't move, the forgiveness we could have allowed ourselves seemed so far away, the hope we should have relied on so impossible.

I said: "So you remember?"

My mother said it was an entertaining film, for children.

"They were digging a grave."

"I don't remember that scene."

"They were supposed to plant a tree, I thought they were getting a place ready for a coffin."

My mother got up from the bed. "It's twenty years ago, why do you still think about it?"

"I always think of the things I remember and also the ones I don't remember: I have space for them, too."

"And you're proud of it? You'll poison yourself, it's not good for you."

"I'm not boasting, I'm saying what I'm like."

"But forget it, Ida, for the love of God, what's the use? It was a good film, a nice evening. And it was so long ago. There was no coffin. You spent an evening watching television with your mother. Is it so difficult for you to have normal memories?"

In front of her I was a defendant who has sworn that he's innocent but acknowledges in himself a vague, unequivocal sense of guilt.

"If you forget, I have to remember doubly. You force me to make a double effort."

"You say you remember everything, but you learn from nothing. I don't forget, Ida. We've already lived like that, with the suffering that you always want to drag out; but everything ends, even suffering. The past is never the same, you can recount it differently after so many years, you know? Maybe you would have liked to see me mourn a man who didn't want us, you would have liked to see me deathly sad. Your father ruined me, but you don't consider that, you care only about yourself, not how I went on, alone. He left, and we'll never know where he went. What people experience in the early days of a relationship has nothing to do with what happens later. Marriage begins when that thing ends. Why did you get married, if you didn't want a child? If you wanted one you should have done it right away. Now you say you don't want one, you've forgotten when you used to say you would call him Sebastiano, like your father."

This, too, was true. In another time, I had been a child hugged by a father, caressing his beard. I had cradled dolls dreaming of a child who would have his name. My mother had held on to that memory and now restored it to me, bright and shiny, just arrived from a time when my father was strong, healthy, and still with us. I would have liked to answer that there would be no Sebastiano, but it wouldn't have been true: a Sebastiano, living or dead, there was and always would be, hidden somewhere or other, his truth unassailable and at the same time defective, like my crumbling certainties.

"So I should have a child, and give him the name of a father who disappeared, a child who will never know if he carries the name of a living man or a dead man. I won't give him a name or even an existence, because as long as the body of my father has no peace, I won't, either," I said all in one breath, bold as a character in a Greek tragedy.

Maybe my mother would have liked to answer, but she had the wit to say nothing. Victorious, I filled the silence by offering to go and get something for dinner, and she said that we had all we needed in the pantry. But I felt like having a beer, the light foamy beer that's made in my city, I wanted to get one directly from the refrigerator of the shop near the house. I needed air, a lot of air, and on the street I breathed oxygen and salt. The shop owner recognized me and greeted me by name, an exaggerated gesture of affection, considering that it came from a coarse old woman so self-satisfied that she had been unable to leave the shop to any of her children, and remained to preside over her kingdom, a kingdom created before I was born. She was exactly the way I remembered her, only with a softer chin and a few more wrinkles. Coming out of her store, I sat on a bench in the old square of Torrente Trapani, recently given over to a playground, drank the first swallow, and thought of Pietro.

A few nights before I left for Messina, we had gone to dinner at our usual restaurant to celebrate the end of my program's summer season. I had ordered fillet and chicory, he a dish of fettuccini, and rather than the usual half bottle of house red, a whole bottle of a Friulian wine. With the first glass I had felt my tiredness relax: I had worked all of August, denying myself beach and vacation, enduring the heat and summer discomforts of Rome, from the mugginess of the subway to the pulled-down shutters. Pietro was talking to me but I wasn't listening, he was complaining about his job and the car that was giving him trouble, he said he wanted to trade it in. Already by the second glass I was more lighthearted, and had extended one foot under the table to poke my husband, trying to play with him as I had during the early days of our acquaintance. He had lowered a hand and tickled one of my ankles; then he stopped and went to the bathroom and I understood that he had gone to wash his hands. His caresses had been affectionate and fun, but the duty of hygiene had called him: we were still at the table, there was still food to touch. I had drowned my disappointment in the third glass, and after dinner in a digestif accompanied by *ciambelline*. Once we were home, in bed, it was he who approached, trying to kiss me without conviction, while I stayed on my side until, almost immediately, he stopped.

Desire isn't made to be patched up: if it's cut off it doesn't recover according to the rules of good manners and the right moment. That was how we lived, every day more fatigued: on the threshold of an elusive, lost desire.

I looked around in the quiet of the afternoon and recognized the slender profile, with long pale curls, that was crossing the street not far from me, speaking cheerfully on the telephone.

"Sara!" I shouted, going toward her happily.

She turned, surprised, and with a nod signaled me to wait until she finished the conversation, then she said goodbye to her interlocutor, promising to call back as soon as possible.

"Hi Ida, how are you?"

"Fine, my mother's doing some work on the house and she asked me to give her a hand, you know, it's full of old stuff, she's making an effort to throw things away."

"How long are you staying?"

"A few more days, my program doesn't go on until October and I'm sort of on vacation. How are you? Do you live nearby?"

"No, I'm up in Annunziata, I bought a place in a new complex, Le Giare. I'm making a house call to a pregnant cat, that's how I end the day."

"You must be the best vet in the city. You live by yourself?"

"I have a beautiful dachshund, Attila."

"Maybe I'll come and see you, we'll have something to eat—what do you say?"

"It's hard these days, Ida, there's too much work, and I'm practically alone in the clinic. Give my best to your mother."

She hadn't asked me any questions, she hadn't talked about my work, she hadn't mentioned the program: did she listen to it? Sometimes, writing, I had mined her life for what I knew. I hadn't had any friends after her, and I realized how much I missed that. Her coldness left a void in my arms, as if I had embraced the air.

A Filipino mother arrived with two little girls, one flung herself onto the swing, the other wanted to play; there was a hopscotch game drawn on the ground in an indelible yellow color. The mother sat on the bench opposite. The older child didn't want to hear of getting off the swing, insistent on rising to challenge the sky, so it was up to me to fulfill the desire of the younger. After an exchange of smiles with the mother I felt authorized to throw the stone first. The child looked at me fearfully, but after seeing me stumble she gathered her courage. I jumped and clenched my teeth so as not to fall retrieving the stone, and I jumped again and again, and then she jumped, I won the first round and the second, I lost the third, and it seemed to me that the day was melting into that scene: two unacquainted girls, one thirty-six and one seven, hopping on one foot, careful not to go outside the lines but always free to laugh, to win, and to lose.

Once I got home, and the heat became less aggressive, I went up to the terrace with my mother. Nikos and his father were working on the parapet.

The sun was setting slightly earlier than the evening before, the days were getting shorter. Nikos gave me a cheerful look and came over.

"So how's the choosing going? Have you decided what to throw away?"

"Actually there's really only one thing that interests me," I said, thinking of my red box.

"Then done, go, go back to your husband, you left him alone for all this time. Didn't you?"

There was a sensual and provocative tone in his voice.

"I'm keeping my mother company until you finish the work. And you said yourself that I ought to be acting like an owner."

"True. And then, best not to trust two men in the house," he sneered.

"Exactly." I looked at the scar on his left cheekbone. Without even making the decision I asked him: "How did you get that?"

He didn't expect the question. He went back to work.

"I'm sorry," I tried to repair things, but he didn't answer. "It's that I don't have friends, I don't talk to anyone. In Rome at least there's my husband, here it's more complicated. Even my mother. Especially her."

My voice trembled and I felt stupid: I must be immensely lonely to be so intimate with a stranger, what could the moods of an older woman matter to him. Nikos examined me again as if I'd said something that concerned him, too.

"It's always complicated to talk to your parents. They're not the right people to understand, and maybe it's easier with someone you don't know."

I thought it would be nice to talk, once, the two of us. Nikos was braver than me.

"What are you doing tomorrow night?"

"Nothing," I said, seizing what seemed to me a promise. "I'm never doing anything."

"Then after work I'll show you something," he said aloud but not too loud, without hiding but still making sure that neither my mother nor his father could hear.

Before going to sleep, before turning off the telephone and charging it, even though the battery was still half full, I read the good-night message from my husband.

The flowered cloth case where I kept the charger was one of the few things I had taken out of the suitcase. I had put it in plain view in an old catchall tray, and when I grabbed it I grazed a carefully folded piece of paper. It was yellowed and creased, but the hand that unfolded it right away was the same as that of the girl who twenty-four years earlier had taken the patient information record out of the trash can, carried it off in her pocket, and shut herself in the school bathroom to read the evidence of her father's illness. It was a novel, in its way: the chapters were the symptoms, the contraindications, and the dosage. Agoraphobia, social anxiety, generalized anxiety: the woman's eyes are the same as the child's, eyes that hadn't needed to read to know.

You take care of Papa's lunch, were my mother's words of goodbye in the morning before she went to the museum. At the time my father still had his job, and a very high-level one was entrusted to me: feeding him. The task of keeping him alive, which my mother, out of fear or incapacity, had already abdicated.

With you he eats willingly, he'll only eat with you, she

said, staring at me, and I remembered when, years before, we'd go to the *passeggiatammare* so that I could practice my skating. Before coming home, we always stopped at the same *rosticceria*. We bought a chicken on the spit and three orders of oven-roasted potatoes, sometimes four, because I couldn't resist that delicious smell, and we ate the first order on a bench facing the sea. Sweaty, not even taking off my skates, I lay with my legs dangling and my head on my father's knees while he put one potato after another in my mouth. Then I chewed and laughed and he laughed with me, and we imitated my mother, foreseeing the moment when, just getting home, she would reproach us for being late and for the suspicion that again, abetted by him, I had eaten outside mealtimes. Now the child is full, she won't want the chicken! she thundered. I was very good at imitating her voice, so good that my father's giant eyes asked for another round: to make fun of her better I got up, swayed on the wheels, put my hands on my hips, and started again.

My father laughed, lit his pipe, asked for an encore.

Only a couple of years later, the scene had changed. My father would return from the Juvarra school with his professor's expression lying heavily on him. In the bedroom he'd take off his shoes and, keeping on pants, shirt, socks, get into his side of the bed. If I looked in to say hello, he answered barely moving his lips, so, in order to avoid not being tolerated, I had stopped even that homage. I stayed on my knees on the chair, leafed through the diary open on the desk, and counted the noises in the other room, which were always the same, soft and cruel: the rustle of clothes and sheets, the thud of shoes, the inescapable sound of aphasia. Those noises now were my father, they enveloped him entirely. He never entered the kitchen, so I got up my courage and went in, crossing the hall like a lizard. Every day, in the oven, in the refrigerator, and on the sink my mother scattered pots and notes with instructions for lunch, it was up to me to carry them out because he wouldn't even look at them.

Papa will only eat with you, she repeated every morning.

Passing his room, I spied through the half-closed door: my father covered up and huddled in the bed, over his ears a pair of headphones attached to the turned-off radio, in his pupils something similar to the water that dripped from the radiators. Meanwhile, outside on the balcony the furnace overheated in an attempt to send steam to the farthest pipes, it gurgled and blew and struggled but in spite of those efforts never managed to reach the rooms at the back of the house, which remained dry, and therefore cold. The driest and coldest was mine. To get warm I took refuge in the kitchen, the epicenter of the house; I put on the pasta water, took out the sauce that my mother had left in a covered casserole in the oven so that it wouldn't attract ants, and after setting the table I sat down to wait for my father. I counted the minutes on the clock and already it was time to turn off the flame, I shook the colander so that the excess water would slide out the holes, I put the red sauce on the orecchiette or fusilli, filled the plates, ate for both, cleared the table, and left the dirty dishes in the sink to show my mother that it had all gone well.

As for me, I had been very good at getting my father and bringing him back among us, a mission I didn't have to give up, since it was so simple?

I performed to the hilt what had to be performed.

Never, not even once, did my father get out of bed to reward me. Never had the shell of unknown thoughts that had become his body considered interrupting the ritual and giving me, his guardian, a prize.

Every day I absorbed the defeat, every day, after the completed performance, I turned back, crossed the hall again, found myself at my father's door and again spied him lying motionless, the switched-off headphones over his ears, the eyes empty, two blankets too many on his thin body, the unperturbed gurgle of water in the radiators. I hurried away as fast as I could, away from the clock case in the hall, from the remains of lunch, from the leftover pasta and tomato in the garbage, away from the responsibility that my mother imposed on me, away from the void in which my father wanted to bury us: to live I had to get to the desk, the desk was salvation, homework a salvation, school and the obligations of the next day were salvation.

My head hurt. I got up and shifted the weight of my body to my toes, I stretched toward the ceiling, my limbs responded unwillingly, my arms, reaching, hurt, my legs pulled. From the wall I heard a gurgle of water.

The radiators were the same as when my father had lived in the house and when he no longer lived there; they had warmed my mother's winters after I abandoned her and would warm the new winter. I didn't know what to do with the objects, but I had no doubt what to do at that moment. Moving aside the wicker basket and a bundle of old magazines, I got down to observe the radiator attached to the wall between the desk and the window: between the narrow tubes dust balls proliferated, infinite nests of old dirt. It had to be cleaned thoroughly, sanitized by scraping away the dirt from the metal folds; it would take proper rags and slim fingers, time and care. I blew and the black cloud of my mother's indolence rose into the air.

I turned the knob on the left side and after a brief silence there was an explosion, as when you open a carbonated drink. The compressed air in the pipes made the water shoot up, and it dripped from the radiator onto my ankles and toes; I had to reclose it and run. Meeting my mother in the hall, I shouted at her with all the voice I had: What have you been doing all these years, what have you taken care of, you haven't bothered with anything.

In the bathroom I found, where it had always been, the purple basin in which I washed and soaped my hands as a child, when I was too short to reach the sink. I took it with me and patiently set to work.

One by one I liberated all the radiators in the house.

I began with my room, collecting the water that was dirty at first and eventually cleaner, jets, and then weaker streams. Then I went to the others: the study, the living room, the hall, the kitchen; when the basin filled up I went to the bathroom, emptied it into the toilet, and flushed, making sure that the dirt of the pipes went down, and disinfecting the bowl every time, as if I had finished, as if I were not about to start again in a new room. My mother followed me in amazement and silence, stunned. "Does it seem normal to you never to have done it?" I couldn't keep myself from attacking her. "Does it seem right to have neglected it?" and I meant the house.

Like a busy cockroach I carried my frenzy to finish from room to room and finally I reached the bedroom, the room closest to the furnace, the room that had suffered the cold least and least needed to be drained, because air hadn't accumulated and the water didn't come out in a torrent as soon as I touched the knob.

I managed to collect only a few drops, so I went to the bathroom for the last time. I put the basin under the open tap, tilting it right and left, I let the running water circulate, cleaning it thoroughly, and I emptied it of the last speck of dirt. It seemed to me that the walls resumed their normal breathing and the house became a body with freed, healed lungs. I went back to bed.

Exhausted, sleepless, I tossed and turned and felt like laughing convulsively. I turned on the phone again and called Pietro. He answered right away: he wasn't sleeping, either. I didn't mention the radiators or my visit to the neighbors, I said I was tired and he told me that in Rome it had rained, he described the beginning of an American film he was watching on television and said for dinner he'd had two rice balls from the pizzeria near work. "Yes, but don't go all these days without cooking something, it's not good for you to always eat takeout food," I told him. He didn't answer. If I appeared worried about his health my husband changed the subject, he wouldn't accept even the possibility that our roles could be reversed: it was he who took care of me; in reality the contrary could also happen, but it remained in the shadows, in mutual silence. It was he, between us, who was supposed to present himself as mother and father. I could accept or reject his care.

I closed my eyes and imagined him.

We were both in bed, each of us alone, in a dark room, half enveloped in warm sheets. We tried to show each other, in words, the day just passed, because we missed each other, but the path between us was interrupted and the sentences couldn't be put in order. I felt worn out and a little dirty, I had skipped dinner with my mother, preferring a chocolate bar, and the tinfoil wrapping and an open bottle of water were near me, lost in the dust and disorder.

"Where are you?" I asked. He, too, must be lying down, with the white T-shirt and blue shorts he always slept in. I sighed, I moaned something intimate and felt I had gained ground. I noticed that our voices changed together, and in the space of a few minutes we began to touch and caress each other, murmuring sweetly, obscenely, on the phone.

In the end we burst out laughing. "Now I have your smell on me," said Pietro. We had never done that, at a distance, on the phone, even though in the first months, after making love, we sometimes spoke about masturbating, as if to let the excitement drain in the thought of a solitary elsewhere, of expectation.

We felt close through a telephone held tight between cheek and shoulder, describing to each other, expressing and allowing intuitions, whispering orders, while when we were in bed together we could no longer cross the few centimeters that separated us. Putting all those kilometers between us had had the opposite effect: the distance had reassured us, creating a new opening.

I heard the volume of the television in our bedroom rise again. Neither Pietro nor I needed to prolong that moment, he wanted to go back to his film and I to my thoughts. We could treat what had happened as a dream; we said goodbye like conspirators and I slid into a light sleep.

Seventh Nocturne

I'm holding a small black kitten in my hands. If you look carefully you see it's not a kitten but a smooth animal without a snout. It has eyes and a nose, and nothing else, it stares at me and would like to speak, if only it could. I caress its head, poor mute kitten, I caress its neck and ears. I caress its smooth, hairless stomach, and realize that it doesn't have genitals. Frightened, I push it away and it leaps but doesn't meow, it bounces off the walls, multiplies infinitely, fills the house, but maybe it's not my house, it's not a nice place, the place where I am.

PART III

The Voice

Unhappiness Wasn't the Rule for All, but Our House Was the Exception

The next morning I turned on the phone again, stared at the battery charging, and waited for the notifications to fill the screen.

The messages that my husband had sent me during the night said this: "I'll join you, Ida. I can't stand it anymore."

Three minutes later: "You're already asleep?"

Six minutes later: "I didn't tell you that water and light arrived today, everything's fine."

I didn't know if I wanted to see Pietro, precisely because sex at a distance had made the night before so unexpected. You can't desire what you already have, while my entire life demonstrated how easy it is to love someone who is absent.

I answered that we had to be patient for just a few more days, and I treasured his messages, postcards from a place where water and light were bills, and to pacify them all you had to do was pay.

◉　◉　◉

"Will you come with me to buy boxes for the stuff you want to save? There's a shop in Tremestieri, it has cardboard or plastic, you can choose."

My mother's voice broke in cheerfully on my breakfast, or maybe it was I who felt happy, after the clandestine and rather dreamlike sex with my husband, like someone who's found a secret in the night and can keep it during the day.

"Mamma, those things in the black bags can be thrown out."

"Then come on, tie them up and we'll throw them out together."

We hadn't gone out together since I arrived. As I climbed into the car I felt like singing, as when we used to drive around, I a girl and she, too, a girl, and I remembered another trip in the car, other garbage.

When my father signed me up for an extraordinary fate, foreseeing my prodigious feet, divine feet, when he saw in me something that wasn't there, wasn't it a declaration of love? In the skates I had trampled the city and its underground ruins, flying over the seabed of the Strait, taking off from the center of the Earth whenever I wanted. It didn't much matter that the announcements of the competitions he mentioned never arrived and that my gifts weren't at all special: I hadn't managed to get beyond the simplest three-turn, barely a dance step, and even that often didn't turn out well. Before our dreams, reality could crouch down on one side, inoffensive. But among the objects that filled my old room, there was no trace of the skates.

Knowing they were in the house was too painful for me, and one day, before one of the drives with my mother, I had put them in a bag of garbage. It was I who stuck my arm out the window toward the trash can, I let go my grip and heard the thud in the container.

A week later I had bought a second-class ticket for Rome, one-way.

When my mother drove up next to a trash bin I felt a pang in my heart and at the same time the need to welcome that pain, tend to it, use it to move past myself and my memories. "I'll get out and throw them in," I offered, picking up the black bags, raising the bar of my resistance as high as I could. She relaxed, satisfied that I was working to help her, while the hard sound of those disused objects repeated a scene I'd already lived.

I went back to the car, my mother turned on the radio, we lowered the windows and started singing.

During the years when we lived by ourselves we had also been happy, in a pure and secret way. Ours was the happiness of the bits of polished glass that children find on the beach, a rare, luminous, and inoffensive happiness; we'd go out with no goal, to flee and cheat the house, we took the highways and the coast roads east toward the Ionian or west toward the Mediterranean, my mother drove and I looked out. When there was rain or sleet, the Strait was filled with waves and the city welcomed us: through the window families and couples went by, lunatics and office workers, people who were sheltering from the rain and people with no home quickening their pace pretending they had one. Every so often we stopped to fill the tank with gas, to check the oil, the tires, to eat the long, thin gelato called *mattonella*, which the baristas cut in slices and served on white plates covered by a tissue paper napkin. The only happiness we were capable of had the short breath of a parenthesis, of an unexpected pause. We never stopped at the sea but traveled alongside it on the highways, and I dreamed of waves long enough to lick the tires of the car, so that I seemed able to swim, to survive.

"Mamma, watch out!" I sat up hard, distracted from my memories when she braked abruptly.

"You want to drive, Ida?"

"No, no. But just because I don't want to drive, it doesn't mean you can do what you want."

"If you want to drive, drive, otherwise be quiet and go along with it."

"Did you renew your license?"

"No, I'm driving without papers. I was waiting for you to remind me, you know."

We continued to provoke each other until we got to our destination, and again in the store, because I found the boxes poorly made and the designs ugly. In the end I chose the least unacceptable, one with red and white stripes and one with big blue polka dots.

"Choose some others, two aren't enough for the things you want to keep."

"But if you sell the house, what does it matter to you?"

"Exactly, say you have to take them to Rome."

On the threshold of indecision we were good. Pretending to discuss the aesthetics or usefulness of objects, we were at rest; we both knew that riling each other was a fiction and hid a peace agreement.

We knew that from other, painful fights in the past.

The year before I moved to Rome we yelled for any reason, and our scenes remained indelible. We argued morning, noon, and night, we fought as if we were invincible and would never die, we fought like eternal beings who could afford the luxury of wasting time; that episodic fight was soon transformed into our only dialogue. The empty refrigerator or the wet clothes neither of us wanted to take out of the washing machine became the pretext for an angry outburst, a game in which we said to each other worse and more, a more outrageous word, an unanswerable insult, a louder cry, a fist against the wall, kicks at the window. I shouted and my mother wept and each of us fielded our most destructive weapon, the most repugnant rage, a curse. One sign of that violence was left: the broken doorknob of my room, the mottled wall around the doorframe, the plaster flaked and fallen. We yelled before and after I'd closed the door, we shouted while I huddled behind it, we shouted and collapsed exhausted. The libation was over, the mutual cannibalism broke off; if it was night I fell asleep in the dark, if it was morning I stared out the window at the world that knew nothing of us.

Of our quarrels there remained neither bones nor dust; I left the house ashamed. The neighbors, I was sure, had heard our shouts and perhaps prayed for us, for the salvation of our souls. The evangelicals never fought: the wall that divided us returned songs and hymns to remind us that unhappiness wasn't the rule for all, but our house was the exception. Once we got home we started again. Tearing each other to pieces was a form of intimacy and for that reason we welcomed it, rather than not know intimacy at all. When we found ourselves alone and felt the itch that would cause us to explode, we experienced the intoxication of the transitory, like couples who go through dinner with the awareness that they will end the evening in bed. Whereas we awaited not love but the fight and, even though we were two, a complete two, covered by one roof, we weren't a couple. We were mother and daughter, and wouldn't have known any other way to mime the absence of my father.

"Ida, I want to tell you something."

"It worries me when you take that tone."

"Listen to me. I know you never listen to me. I also know you like to do the opposite of what I tell you, you have your own ideas, let's not repeat what we've already said, but will you listen to one thing from your mother? You can't make life out of remnants, with what you keep in reserve. You don't have another life, a provisional one, where you can put the things you don't do."

"So?"

"When your father got sick, it's true, I tried to stay away from him as much as I could. You think I neglected him. I'm not excusing myself. I was young, I had a job I liked, I had you, I was worried about you."

"And you entrusted him to me every day."

"I was wrong with you, not with him. His illness exasperated me, I would have covered your eyes with my own hands if I could. I didn't want you to see him or us like that. But I didn't know how, I couldn't manage it. You don't know what it means to have a child and be unable to protect her. Happiness is important, Ida."

"Don't start again with what I can't understand, talk about yourself, when you talk about yourself you're less pathetic."

"Ida, how you speak to your mother. What?"

"Shall we stop and get some *mattonella*?"

At that moment I would have torn the seat belt to pieces, I needed air, my mother's sincere words struck me more than her accusations.

Happiness doesn't exist but happy moments do: we had taken care of the box store early, it wasn't even nine-thirty in the morning, and before going home, sitting outside at our favorite *pasticceria*, we stole another one.

Here's what I had been good at until that moment: not falling. At thirteen, after my father's disappearance, in order to live, I should have invented myself. The way others construct their body, muscle after muscle, with practice and athletics, or sculpt their mind and intelligence through psychoanalysis, culture, or meditation, the way they carve a triceps in the gym or unearth a tendon they didn't even know they had, the way they find a job, the necessary salary, the safe seat, the degree, the pose for the passport photo, the posture that fits their character, the dress that seems sewed on—in other words, in the same way that all invent who they are and by inventing it assert themselves, in that same way it was up to me.

But I didn't know who I was. What had happened to me concerned me, but it had happened when I was too young for the world to recognize it in me. People wouldn't stop time and their own habits, we would all go forward, because the planet is full of disasters, wars and hunger and rapes, and if a teacher comes down with sadness it's his own fault, he failed to protect wife and daughter from external attacks and even from himself. What sort of man could a man like that be? He didn't even care about the child, whispered the silence of the city; or maybe the city didn't care about me, my father, or our family—that was the most likely hypothesis. My mother and I were two birth certificates and one day we would be two death certificates, and in the middle two votes, two wills, finally a distant legend: Look, two women lived in that house, the citizens would say to each other, passing under my balcony. Or we would be nothing, not even ghosts of a legend, and after us another family would buy the house and make it a different place. Then you'd open the door and breathe in a fresh normality, there would be sounds of children and toys, polished furniture and painted walls, an efficient washing machine, a calendar, a small blackboard and colored chalk in the kitchen, as the evangelicals had; my life and my mother's would be covered over, would have died with us, because new, legitimate owners would buy our walls and the right to sweep us away.

I thought of this on the last stretch of the way home, while from the window I looked for the sea of my childhood. If I wanted to live, I had to cross that sea and not stop: my place wasn't Scylla or Charybdis and maybe it didn't exist on any map, certainly it wasn't a question of kilometers. That was why, years earlier, Rome had seemed to me the most suitable: the biggest city, the strongest, surrounded by walls. I had to flee, enter the Urbe on horseback like a conqueror and turn, look at Sicily with the distance of a telescope and the assurance of a refugee, and then forget myself and mingle with the tourists of Piazza Navona, with the tramps at Termini station, with the flower pots on the bourgeois balconies of the residential neighborhoods. Every atom of me was made of the air of the house in Messina, and for that reason I would have to leave it. Some things would follow me like dogs, tokens of misery and fate, but once safe I would tame them, make them harmless, far from the house I would be naked, light, and free. That's what I thought at twenty.

So I continued to wonder who I was, while my mother parked and we took the boxes we'd just bought out of the trunk.

I was the child born of a man and a woman who had loved each other for a short time, the guardian of my father's depression, my mother's angry daughter, the patient and deserving student, the frightened young woman. Every day I learned to hide the shame and put on strength like a sailor, to command from a corner the way women command. My mother and I were a family as if nothing had happened, but we were also special because unspeakable things had happened to us.

The passage of time remained for me a great hardship.

Forever and Ever (Like a Nocturne)

The telephone rings in the middle of the night, I get up sleepy and frightened, an unknown male voice is calling me: "Signorina Ida Laquidara? I have a message for you. Do you know a man by the name of Sebastiano?"

"He's my father," I answer, opening my eyes.

"He's here with me, he's asking for you, he's lost his memory but today he remembered this telephone number and your name . . ."

Repeat.

The telephone rings in the middle of the night, I get up sleepy and frightened and a voice with a foreign accent speaks in a hurry: "Signorina Ida Laquidara? Excuse the time, I'm calling from Lebanon. Do you know that your father, a man of forty-seven by the name of Sebastiano Laquidara, made a journey here alone?"

The voice stops to let me absorb the blow, my father left, he died from a sudden illness, the body has to return to Italy.

Repeat.

I come home from school in the afternoon, my mother is waiting for me in the doorway in tears, with her coat and purse, standing next to the blue stool. They've called from the police station, my father's body has been washed up by the sea, a fisherman from Torre Faro found it on the beach. Mamma, Mamma, I cry, hugging her, we get in the car, I drive. "At least I can say goodbye to the body of the man I love," my mother whispers, or maybe my thoughts are speaking, I clutch her hand, I turn on the windshield wipers to wash away the rain, I change gears, I look for parking, I support my mother, I support the world, I don't collapse, I never collapse.

Repeat.

I come out of school with my backpack on, the way I did in elementary school, and, as I did then, I turn and see my father whole, standing near the entrance, he's drumming his fingers and he smiles at me in that slightly mad way of his, what a trick he played on us! He'd been there all along, hadn't we seen him, how could we believe that he had really gone away? Had we really worried so much?

Everything is true in my fantasies, everything is absolutely present. My father killed himself in the sea, my father died while trying to remake a life for himself in a foreign country, my father is alive right before our eyes, my father was seized against his will, he went out to take a walk but would have come back, my father had a heart attack, an aneurysm, a traffic accident, my father had another woman, also another child, my father returns after a year, two years, five years.

Living or dead, my father comes home, he has a voice again, a body, a name. I construct other existences and new stories, I carve out a parallel world in which voices, bodies, and names are in motion, well articulated, divided into syllables, and concrete. My imagination has no limits: it's not true. My imagination is an alert dictator, and if there's a contradiction it brakes, shies, Correct it! It orders me, Correct it! It shouts, Correct it! Everything has to be perfect, everything, correct! For years I obey every night, every night I submit, I add details, I eliminate inconsistencies, I blur what doesn't work, I add what I know, even during the day I am employed by my nighttime dictator: What sort of government is there in Lebanon? What color is the boat of that fisherman on the beach at Torre Faro? An instant, an instant.

Every night, for years, I tell myself the story, I tell it better. Because my father is alive and wants to return, my father was kidnapped, my father died by mistake, my father went to die in the place that most belonged to him: the water. My father hugs me, holds me tight, asks my forgiveness, doesn't ask me anything and is presumptuous, amazed: were we really worried by his absence? My mother weeps, suffers, broods, hugs my father's body, the living body, the dead body, finally in a mortuary chapel, lying on marble, wrapped in a sheet, put in a sack. My mother looks at me with love, with anger, with attention: she looks at me with eyes that let me exist. Every night I take advantage of my insomnia to elaborate a more effective, more realistic story; but imagination doesn't fire up, nor do memories. Imagining is of no use, except to make the waiting time pass, my father may return, he will return to this house and no other, but did a man really exist whom

I called father? Why were we resigned to his disappearance, why didn't we fight, why didn't we sense that he was alive, without memory or confused, lost or isolated, but alive? The relatives of people who disappear usually have premonitions, certainties, strong sensations of presence—not us. I was used to staying in my shadow and in my father's, occasionally receiving an object, a feeling, a caress, a testimonial of the world outside; but nothing, not even objects, not even evidence—a receipt, a letter, a diary, a pack of cigarettes, a pair of skates—can prove that an event staged in the mind really happened. My father turns off the alarm clock, chooses the tie, looks at the toothpaste on the sink like the slimy trail of a snail—that, at least, happened?

Objects aren't reliable, memories don't exist, only obsessions. We use them to keep the crack open and we tell ourselves that memory is important, that we alone are its guardians. We keep the wound wide so that our troubles and our fears fit in it, we make sure it's deep enough to contain our suffering, you mustn't let that get away.

Only obsessions exist, and meanwhile time has made them truer than we are.

"Ida?"

My husband, the voice I was looking for, answered right away.

"Ida, are you all right?"

"Pietro, please, listen to me."

"Where are you?"

"I'm not well. I made a mistake. Too many things . . . With my mother, nothing is solved. She put all the stuff in my room. I don't know how to explain it to you, it gives me the impression of death, it's a nightmare."

"Ida, where are you?"

My husband's voice was strong and warm, it was curative thermal water, in the background was a foreign woman speaking English, I couldn't catch the phrases, only words like *economy* and *buildings* and *politics*; my husband was improving his English in the car, on the way to work, the recorded voice read articles and asked him questions, urging him to comment. It pretended to ask his opinion as if it were really important that he have an idea on the subject, as if he weren't simply making an effort to express some opinion, because it was the exercise that counted. I listened to the woman speaking, and felt affectionate toward my husband: English was of no use to him, was of no use for anything, but the commute in the car could be unbearable, no one wants to be stuck with his thoughts all that time.

"How was work today?"

Lawyers, Europe, commission. Pietro turned off the radio and didn't consider it necessary to answer me.

"I'll come get you, I'll take the highway, Ida, I knew you were making a mistake."

"No, no. I'm fine. I'm home."

"Is your mother with you?"

"She's in the other room. The workers are here."

"You're in your room?"

"It's the usual story of my father, but my mother has piled up everything in here—you know, she's emptying the house and I'm afraid of the objects, they're giving me a mean look."

"You're very strong, Ida. Stop brooding, you're not your

mother, remember that, you're not her. I let you go because you had to give her a hand. Choose the things you want to keep, tell her what to throw away, in fact the two of you throw it away together, and then come home."

Without the English woman Pietro's car was occupied by silence, he must have pulled over to talk to me more easily. I imagined him with his hand still on the wheel, my voice filling the space. I was silent, too.

"Ida. You understand, you're not your mother. I'm coming to you. I can't today or tomorrow, because I'm substituting for a colleague, but I'll leave in two days and be with you."

My husband's voice caressed my hair, smoothed the folds in my neck, brushed the space between the nape and the ears. I ended the conversation, held the telephone in my hands, and thanked the technological miracle that allowed one to be invaded by another person hundreds of kilometers away, to have one's mood altered by him, and to ask him to help one resist.

I took an old pair of light jeans out of the closet and a white ribbed shirt that resembled the workers'.

Lamps

Happiness doesn't exist but happy moments do. With Pietro's warm voice still in my ears, I went up to see if I could get in advance that other moment I was entitled to.

Nikos and his father were working quickly in the sun, overwhelmed by the din of metal and pipes and tools, shouting tersely from one end of the roof to the other in a mixture of dialect and Italian. As soon as they became aware of my presence they stopped talking but not working, and neither of them came toward me. I went over to Nikos, who was adjusting the base of a lamp. My mother had wanted eight lamps along the sides of the terrace, for when it got dark, maybe to have parties if she didn't succeed in selling the house right away, and I had thought that even if she never sold it, even if I spent much more time there than usual, we would never have parties on the terrace, because we never did things like that together, and because nothing is more melancholy than a summer party.

Once, Sara and I had been invited by a boy in our class to his birthday party. It was before the day at Scylla. Sara was already going out with Fabio but hadn't brought him with her, and we arrived at a sumptuous apartment, with a long double living room, hanging lamps, and small crystal objects in display cabinets along the walls. On the tables were trays of Messinese focaccia (cut-up tomato, escarole, cheese, some with anchovies and others without) and lots of ice-cold beer. We weren't many, since the majority had already left with their parents for their second houses at the beach, and we ate and drank and chattered. Then the boy's mother came in, asking if everything was all right, without hiding a worried expression. And she told us what had just happened: a thief, trying to get in through the window of an apartment on the top floor, had slipped and fallen into the light well, and had died instantly. The mother, frightened, added that an ambulance had come to take away the thief, and, finishing her story, closed the door as if she wanted to protect us. For a moment the noise of us young people had been suspended, then it resumed as if nothing had happened, and I went out on the balcony, which faced the street. Leaving behind the heedless voices of my classmates, especially those of Sara and the birthday kid, I observed the street, dark in spite of the lights of the ships and smaller boats, feeling that nothing could be sadder than this: a summer evening in a city that has emptied out, a man who dies setting his foot in the wrong place, a group of teenagers continuing to celebrate a birthday. I went back into the living room, and the anguish passed, or maybe it was transformed into something else.

◎   ◎   ◎

Nikos was fumbling with one of the lamps my mother wanted, he stopped and looked at me.

"Shall we go?" I said.

"Now I'm working."

"Come on, let's go now," I repeated, "it's hot for work."

Signor De Salvo had stopped, too, and was looking at me with a questioning expression.

"I'm taking Nikos for a walk," I shouted, forcing myself to be friendly.

"Signora, I'm sorry, but without my son I can't finish putting up the lamps and the work will come to a halt."

"We'll never use them. We won't have any parties on this terrace, I don't live here and my mother doesn't invite people over—these lamps are useless, no one will ever light them."

"This afternoon I have to set them up again. And then, if I may: you don't know what your mother will do on this terrace, you children think you know everything."

We are also responsible for what we didn't want to see, I thought. I was, too. What did others see in my mother's life, beyond and after my father? Who was that small-boned, severe-looking woman, sensual in her harshness? I remembered the months of the Miser, a man my mother had gone out with for a short time six years after my father's disappearance, a store owner whom I immediately hated, and I had fed that hatred by concentrating on his flaws, the worst of which was stinginess. I couldn't tolerate his tense face the moment the bill arrived, I couldn't tolerate the calculations he made about the price of everything. I was nineteen, and stinginess seemed to me the worst quality in a man. I imagined my mother calling the Miser again and welcoming him to the terrace in the light of the lamps that had just been set up: on a swing, or under a gazebo, they would drink coffee and talk about old times, looking at the ferries docking and departing and at Calabria cloud-covered or clear, always too near or too far.

"Come on, it doesn't make any difference. It doesn't make any difference if you continue the work this afternoon," I insisted.

The Miser and my mother had gone out for a few months, during which I adopted small stratagems of attack. When they came to pick me up at my university classes, or gave me a ride from one part of the city to another, when I saw them together, sitting in our car—ours: mine and my mother's—I felt a mounting rage for the violated triangle: my mother, my father, me; or: my mother, the house, me; or: my mother, the car, me. I dismissed the fact that new ones could be born, or that the triangle could become a quadrilateral. What did the Miser have to do with us, sitting on the throne in front, which pushed me to the rear again, forcing me into the back seat? He got out to welcome me and greet me, because the car didn't have four doors, and to get in I had to slide behind the front seat, lifted up and leaning toward the windshield. The Miser got out, accommodating, to let me get in, and for him it was a triumph, whereas for me—who had to bend my back, crouch down, and crawl through the door—there was shame and humiliation, expulsion from the kingdom. Our car—without a doubt: ours—then became an occupied territory, and, huddled behind him, in a sign of protest I pushed my knees against his seat back to annoy him. My mother wasn't aware of it, the Miser took it and adjusted his position, but there was nothing he could do: my legs, ready for the fight, aimed at his spinal column, went on pressing, and pressing, and pressing against the seat at the height of his bones. I would have pierced them if I could, boring into his sternum; for my enemy there was no salvation. I pushed and pushed, angrily, and it seemed to me that I saw him sweat, defending his position with a show of indifference; he would never allow himself to scold the daughter of his lover, and even to complain would have been a serious mistake: if he had reported that my knees were sticking into his back like bayonets, he would have lost forever the possibility of an alliance. When he finally got out of the car, because we had arrived or because I had arrived, I read in his face a tortured relief. The battle was over and I had won; losing the war no longer mattered to me. But I won that, too; at a certain point the romance was over and he disappeared from our days. He had asked her to live with him, but my mother had ruled out that possibility, either in our house or elsewhere, making it in fact a story without a future. It had been her most effective form of care for me.

"Anyway, this house is mine, too," I said to Nikos and his father, resigning myself to going down the stairs alone, and yet not wanting to give up on a late-morning walk.

Annunziata

Messina's cool morning air was giving way to the heat of the sun as it grew stronger. At first I thought of going to the cathedral, where every day at noon the clock spectacle starts up: the lion roars, Dina and Clarenza, the protectors of the city, ring the bells, the rooster crows, Death, with his scythe, marks the four stages of life: childhood, youth, maturity, old age. I liked the idea of returning to the square and half closing my eyes while the Schubert "Ave Maria" began. In high school the teacher would open the window and we students sat still and quiet, ears straining: on days when the wind was favorable, the noon sounds and music from the cathedral reached the school and our developing minds. At the university I'd kept up the habit, looking out between classes, waiting for the notes of the toy clock; if I was out walking, I'd manage to end up in front of the cathedral, I'd mingle with the tourists and impatiently observe the bell tower until the short and long hands were superimposed. Midday could then release its magic.

I headed toward the center anticipating a renewal of that solitary joy, but everywhere, in the cars and at the tables of the cafés, I saw mothers and fathers, couples and single parents who, having taken their children to school, were stealing, with one coffee and another, a shred of late-morning freedom before going to work. Again I saw my father when he took me to elementary school and then went on to the Juvarra, and my mother the rare times she brought me and continued on to the museum; I felt such nostalgia, regret for a time that couldn't return, that I turned my eyes toward the sea.

But the water didn't respond. And I was seized by a great desire to react, to be born again, to pummel life, immerse myself in the present if only to resolve at least one of my disrupted stories. Maybe my mother was right, it didn't make sense to spend all day reversing course toward the past. No matter how much power we attribute to our thoughts, they won't alter what happened. I would go to the coast, choose a modest beach, and go swimming. A swim. Long, liberating, purifying. By myself, though, I wouldn't make it, the memory of the dream of the night before leaving was too vivid, the fear too present. I would be able to swim if someone was on the shore waiting for me, and there was one person in the city I would have liked to play that role: Sara.

Gathering my courage, I climbed up the vertical line of the *torrenti*, headed for the neighborhood of Annunziata. It was a risk: climbing up and not finding her, because she was at work. Or, worse, finding her and feeling again the chill she'd shown at the playground. Part of me knew that Sara was certainly not dying to see me. But I was dying to see her, and I relied on what I needed.

I took the risk.

To the right and left I passed the tall apartment blocks built some decades ago, new homes that claimed to dominate the city. Going up higher, I observed houses with gardens that would never be seen in the center, houses where you could sit peacefully outside on summer evenings, in tranquility after sunset, and the city, seen and imagined, began to look tiny: the sickle-shaped harbor and the Strait, the top of the bell tower, the small boats and the Caronte ferries, the light of Scylla and the shadows of Charybdis, the line of cars stopped at the intersections, the scattered gardens of dry green, the hazy curtain of Torrente Boccetta, carrying the trucks that supplied the island with imported goods and exported as many when they left—from above the whole made up an alien relief map, a reduction in scale of the place where I had lived. I knew the city by heart, but I never looked at it like that; was that how Sara saw and imagined it, from above?

Arriving at the gate of the Le Giare complex, I looked for her name among the buzzers, and reading it I felt an uncontrollable turmoil. We were no longer friends, Sara and I.

Our relationship had ended on the threshold of twenty, summed up in the mutual gaze of two involuntary witnesses who no longer wanted that role. Each looking onto the other's life, we had been girls as best we could, or, rather, we had passed through the worst age, adolescence, on parallel paths from which every so often we held out a hand to each other.

"Who is it?"

"Hi, Sara. Am I disturbing you?"

We were now two adult voices talking through an intercom.

It would have been ridiculous to make an excuse, to say that I was passing by; no one wanders randomly through the complexes of Annunziata.

"Ida. I'm on my way to work, wait a second, I'm coming down."

Sara had recognized me immediately, but she wouldn't let me enter her house. The chill in her voice reminded me of what I had suspected: while I had recovered memories of tenderness, she offered me a polite but firm distance.

The front door opened. Sara, in a purple cotton dress, her feet in a pair of flat leather sandals, came toward me. She stopped between the entrance and the gate, smoothed her hair, looked for something in her purse, and, raising her head, clenched her teeth while I couldn't restrain an expression of victory. I would have liked to go through the bars, rush up to her and hug her tight, wrinkle her dress, muss her hair, tell her she was beautiful and together find a way back, for both of us, into our shared history; but from her came a distinct coolness.

"Sara, I'm sorry."

"Don't worry," she answered impatiently, passing through the gate. "I'm late, I should have started early today. It's hot—did you walk up?"

"Yes, sorry. The name of the complex struck me, Le Giare. It's a sort of melancholy day and I thought: maybe you'd feel like going to the beach, we could stop at my house, I'll get my bathing suit . . ."

"No, Ida, it's impossible, I have to go to work. I don't have time to relax, today will be a crazy day at the clinic. But if you want I'll take you home, I have to go down that way, too."

I followed her to the garage; she had taken the keys out of her purse. She warmed up the engine, brought out one of those small fashionable cars my husband called "tunafish cans," and opened the door, apologizing for its untidiness.

"I never have time to clean it," she explained, more to herself than to me, and getting in I felt something familiar: we nest only in dirty places, I recalled.

Inside her car Sara seemed more relaxed, she felt protected, as I'd once felt in my mother's and my car; but she placed her hands on the steering wheel skillfully and I couldn't stop admiring her, grateful to the fate that had led her to find me as the friend of adolescence. Sara's voice, aspect, closeness were a gift, even at the cost of the cold bark I had to tolerate to enjoy it. Driving with the assurance of someone performing a daily ritual, she guided the car out of the garage and through the gate, and turned onto the steep descent that would take us back to the flat neighborhoods.

While I was spellbound by the confidence with which Sara handled her car, my father stood out before me with a new clarity. Not his ghost in the form of water but an almost real creature.

My father came up from the sea and walked, barefoot, in the middle of the street, in the opposite direction from ours, wearing clothes tattered by the waves and encrusted with salt, the blue jacket that would be fashionable throughout the decade following his disappearance, and which he—already broken and battered but attached to his own bursts of vanity—had bought before going to bed and not getting up again. It was that detail that inspired a sudden new fear: the jacket hadn't changed, it was the same, with slightly rounded sleeves and elastic wristbands, elastic at the neck. Fashions changed, but not the jacket.

She doesn't get older, I repeated to myself, referring to the girl living inside me who had stopped at thirteen.

She doesn't change, said my father's jacket.

What isn't transformed isn't real; nothing, in my life, was transformed.

I looked at Sara. Absorbed in driving, she had turned on the radio and was listening to the news.

"Sara . . ."

I thought: Did you see him, too? Did you, too, always see him when you came to study at my house and my father was still there, in the form of damp stains on the ceiling, water that wouldn't go away?

"What, Ida."

I thought: I can't make it. I'm in Sicily, it's September, it's as hot as midsummer, but I don't have the strength to go in the water without you nearby. What's happening to me?

"I don't feel like going to the beach. Not by myself."

"I'm sorry, Ida, I really can't."

I thought: So it seems like a whim, and Sara will move even farther away from me, but she doesn't want to listen to me, she wants to go to work. And I just saw my father, I saw him.

To emerge from the stupor that vision had put me in, I asked: "How's it going at the clinic?"

My voice was shaking, but Sara didn't notice. She complained about her inexpert and inadequate colleagues, their reckless arrogance that endangered the lives of the animals, the unhygienic conditions she had to reproach them for, about cats, dogs, canaries, the absurd egocentric pretensions of owners of exotic animals. Oozing from every phrase was how superior she felt to her surroundings, how wasted she felt in the provincial clinic. All those words at least had the effect of calming me. The university, she said, hadn't been able to guarantee her a job in spite of her top grades, and she had had to abandon research to get locked into a job that wasn't satisfying. Luckily there was Attila, the dachshund, who waited for her every day, but he was a problem, too, because Sara got home late and never had time to take him out—

"Like your neighbor's dog, who barked when it was alone," I interrupted her.

"What?"

"That's what you always told me when you came to my house to do homework, the owner went out and the dog barked, so you couldn't sleep."

"I don't remember. Anyway my mother goes to Attila, which breaks up his day, and she takes him out before I get home."

We insist on considering memory a cake that can be shared, and we never resign ourselves to the fact that a fact isn't a fact isn't a fact—a rose isn't a rose isn't a rose, contrary to what our high school teacher taught us to write in our notebooks. No, a fact isn't a fact: it's perhaps a detail that we accentuate for a moment, through suffering or our solipsistic tendency to turn in on ourselves. A detail seen or heard, which immediately becomes material for our unconscious and for our drives, one element in a series of preceding and successive details. Had the dog that disturbed

Sara's peace as a girl really existed, the dog that, in the years after my father's disappearance, I envied for the capacity to cry that I lacked? Sara—who became a vet and who, as a girl, was already attentive to the faintest signal from the animal world—didn't even remember it.

"I missed you madly when we stopped hanging out together. Sometimes I think I went to live in Rome because it made no sense to stay in the same city as you if I couldn't see you, listen to you. I said to myself that it was a glorious natural end, but the truth is that I suffered, I always had a million things to tell you, I still do. You were the only person my mother and I had over. I wasn't comfortable in my house, it's a damp house, suspended in time. I missed my father, I was afraid of people. I trust you, period; how many letters I wrote you, I have yours here, in the house in Messina, I wrote them in pen, you remember the green pen? Do you still have yours? I never again had a pen like that one. I still write stories for the radio—I make up stories about people who don't exist. The program is on the air every day, I don't know if you've ever listened to it. In the second year of university you had that tall friend, from Reggio Calabria. I saw you together in the city center, on Saturdays, and I envied her because she could spend time with you. I've been here for days, and no one knows me like you, my mother's on my back, my husband's in Rome."

"Don't apologize, Ida, but for me, really: nothing happened."

"Maybe that's the point, for me everything happened."

"You know why we stopped seeing each other, Ida?"

Now we had descended too far, the sea was no longer visible. The smell of Sara's hair pervaded the car, a citrus smell, the same shampoo she'd used in high school.

"Your problems don't justify everything, you're not the only one who exists in the world," she continued, stopping the car at a red light.

Leaving Annunziata behind us, we had entered the flow of the city, the hum of stores, people, pedestrian strips. "I would have liked to say this to you and I'll say it now: You never opened up, I know it was difficult, I mean the story of your father and the rest. But I had my problems, too, maybe they didn't seem as important to you as yours. I loved you and I still do, but in our friendship there was only you. Other people's suffering exists, too, Ida."

I would have liked to plug up my ears, rewrite the conversation, putting different words in Sara's mouth. I would have liked to shout that's not true, but Sara had her view, which also explained precisely the way she behaved, not avoiding me but not encouraging closeness, not even to celebrate the past. A fact isn't a fact but a gaze is a gaze: hers on me had been privileged. Whether I liked it or not, it was our closeness that produced her detachment.

I listened to Sara's voice, a clear adult voice; it wasn't a sandstorm unleashed by my mother or the hospitable bed with which Pietro had welcomed me on the telephone. A voice mindful of the words it chose.

"Ida, do you remember the day you came to the hospital?"

We were nineteen when Sara had an abortion. It hadn't happened to me, it had happened to her: and that made the difference. If the most untruthful sentence in any dialogue is "I understand you," that episode doomed any possibility of communication between us. It was her body, not mine. Not for an instant had Sara wanted to keep the baby, which wasn't Fabio's or that of the boyfriend after Fabio, it was the child of a stranger, of an encounter similar to the one I myself had had on the beach at Scylla, and, later, other times, single and occasional, sufficient to be sure that if it had happened to me, I wouldn't have kept the child, either, and in fact we wouldn't even have kept a child conceived during a lasting romance, because we ourselves were still children and at nineteen we wanted to be everything except mothers. But it hadn't happened to me, it had happened to her.

"So, Ida, do you remember or not?"

If it happens to the body it didn't really happen: I must have used my mantra that afternoon, too, sitting next to Sara, who was staring into space, and we talked a little and I read to her a little and she listened; I had with me some magazines and a book by Henri Alleg, *The Question*, because after Camus I was obsessed with the French, so I told her, saturating the silence with my nineteen-year-old student's verbosity as I reflected on political power and the oppression of prisoners, on how many prison camps had the right to call themselves "place of command" and how it wasn't simple to identify only one such place; and I talked, giving myself the illusion of diminishing the distance between us, between what had happened to her and what had not happened to me. But preparing to mark an abandonment means confirming that that abandonment has already taken place, and it had been a long time since Sara and I had been the same people who mirrored each other at the high school desk, we weren't the girls who spent long afternoons studying together.

"When you came to see me. Don't misunderstand, it was right for you to be there. I couldn't have tolerated anyone else."

After she had an abortion and I didn't, we separated forever. We were already distant, but after that episode we could no longer pretend or minimize. In the beginning, at fourteen, she had living parents and I the stump of a family, but at the time the difference had solidified our bond. So we had met, two bits of wreckage that wouldn't sink.

"You were the only one who knew about the abortion. You were always the only one, Ida. I was flattered to be your friend, you were the most intelligent in the class, you must have been at the university, too, and I'm sure you are in your job as well. No, I don't listen to your program. At that hour I'm at the clinic. But I imagine that you found peace getting away from here, being far away from your mother. Whereas I stayed, you know what that means, right? You're too intelligent not to know."

Before she went to the hospital Sara told her parents that she was going with me to Etna for a couple of days, we would go hiking and sleep in the hostel at Zafferana. I said nothing to my mother, she didn't ask questions and didn't talk to other mothers, it wouldn't be a problem to spend the time at the hospital, occupy the visiting hours, hang around the waiting room and talk to the doctors to be sure that everything went well. At most, if I was late getting home, we'd find some pretext for fighting, blind behind our insults.

"Maybe you knew even better than I did how I felt before the abortion, how I would feel after. It's true, a terrible thing had happened to you before we met, you were a child, your father shouldn't have disappeared like that, I don't have to tell you. He was a coward, weak, you don't leave a wife and a daughter without explanation and with that burden. For years I said to myself that one can't judge without taking account of others' fragility, including his, and that basically he had left you this: your acuteness, you're as sensitive as a seismograph. But also your blindness. We're all fragile, Ida, you more than anyone. You allowed your suffering to devour you, and your wound became bigger than you. You live like a slave, you're the slave of what happened to you—you were like that at fourteen, too, and you made me your fellow slave. Suffering made you fascinating, but you didn't realize it, you didn't see anything, you never really saw me. But I was there, I was always beside you and I didn't ask any questions, we never talked about your father. I didn't even know his name, I didn't dare ask you."

Heedless and majestic, the city continued on its course outside the window.

"I endured your dictatorship for years, and not to say you knew it, I know you weren't aware of it. But when I had the abortion I couldn't stand it anymore, I had changed. I didn't say anything to you, but after the operation the doctors explained that I couldn't have children, something was wrong with my uterus. I had to wait to have the tumor removed, have tests and then the other operation, this time with my mother, and then it was me who decided not to talk to anyone about it, especially not you. Meanwhile we had already lost each other. When you came to see me in the hospital, and I repeat, I thank you because you were the only person I wanted, you started piling up words, burying the truth. You scared me. You seemed like your mother and I realized you'd become like her, a woman who lives around a bleeding cut, even when the blood has dried, the scab crumbled and fallen off. How could I share something with you, sitting there reading, talking to me nonstop about your books or the nonsense in the newspapers? Even my abortion was becoming a phobia of yours. I don't know why you came today, there's no need for us to spend time together anymore. What do you want from me? If you need something I'm here, if you need me I'll help you, but I don't need to see you again: I know who you are, Ida."

It was a few blocks to my house, and with relief I thought: mine. Sara's suffering had filled the car. And yet it hadn't surprised me. Part of me knew: as long as she didn't have suffering of her own she had been able to tolerate mine, then something had occupied the space, kicking me out. Her estrangement was a defense, the boundary on which she had built her adulthood, and there was no longer a place to welcome me, not even years later. So I stayed apart, not out of fear but because that suffering had no need of my presence.

"I would have liked you to meet my husband, Pietro. But he doesn't like coming to Messina. He doesn't like the sun, and then he doesn't know how to swim."

"You're with someone who's afraid of the water?" Sara laughed. "You, really you. You spent hours in the sea."

"I must have gotten that habit from my father. He also liked it a lot."

"Whereas your mother, never seen on a beach."

"She did go. You remember when we took the ferry to Scylla with Fabio?"

"What was it, the summer we were sixteen? You had a really great two-piece bathing suit."

"The beach was white, who knows what it's like now. At some point you left me alone. I'd come with you, but I ended up alone all afternoon."

"I'm sorry. Fabio was a shit, if I think what an idiot I was. What did you do?"

"Nothing. I went swimming."

I lied to protect her, or to mark for myself the distance that now separated us, and perhaps had always been there.

We drove a few hundred meters, until she stopped the car in front of my building, double-parking without turning off the engine, so I obeyed her expectations and said goodbye. Sara went off to her job, hidden behind her explanations, and I understood what I had missed: learning to say goodbye. We love our obsessions, and we don't love what makes us happy, on the contrary. We cling to each other, and none of us are made of noble substances.

Before going home, I decided to walk some more; I had in my nostrils the clean, orange smell of Sara's hair when I arrived at the Caronte bar. I ordered a coffee and sat near the windows, observing the ferries that docked and set out. That foreign land called the suffering of others really did exist; that suffering was equal to ours and at the same time completely unknown. What Sara felt had exiled her from me; I would have liked to go back and remove that weight from her future, take away the curse of an impossibility. Neither she nor I had had children, but I had been able to choose and she hadn't, and that detail made the difference. As for the words she had used to describe me, they concerned me up to a certain point; our friendship was extinct, dried out like the edges of towels that succumb to salt water and the August sun, while Sara needed to make them into a theory of my character. Her words contained a truth, but she had neglected to say that our bond would probably have dissolved anyway. Maybe from that torrent of sentences I would extract the ingredients for one of my radio stories, because she was right, I could tolerate suffering only by writing about it, and by transforming it into an invention I could find the peace that was absent from daily life. I put down the cup and continued to stare outside until my father appeared again.

This time he had his back to me and went into the water toward the deeper sea, toward the Calabrian coast that seduced him like a song. He returned to his element; feet, knees, hips were submerged, and then his whole self, in the unfashionable jacket, and walking toward the peninsula, he sank down deeper and deeper, until nothing remained of his body, his back, his neck, and the water closed over the last lock of his hair. In his place a long stain formed and the whirlpool slowed, replaced by a group of bubbles that became sparser until they vanished.

The sea was smooth again.

I looked frantically for the phone in my purse, I found three calls from Pietro, and again I felt like hearing his voice.

"I saw Sara," I started off, walking toward home.

"How are you? Your voice is strange."

I thought: I saw my father.

"She explained why our friendship broke off"—the cars were flowing on one side of me, the sea on the other. "From her point of view, I mean."

"OK. Was it useful to you?"

"I don't know. Pietro?"

"What is it, Ida? Why are you feeling so bad?"

"It must be the confusion in the house, or the work, or the heat, but I see my father everywhere."

"I know. And you know something, I don't know what to do. I feel useless, so far away."

He didn't understand, and that, too, basically calmed me.

"Come soon. If you're here it'll be better."

Before going home I stopped at a takeout food shop and ordered eggplant and pepper *involtini* stuffed with bread, garlic, and cheese, two servings of cooked greens, and one of roasted potatoes. I pointed with my finger to a whole wheat baguette made according to an ancient recipe, and didn't refuse when the girl behind the counter offered to stick napkins and plastic utensils in the bag, as if I were going to eat outside, on a bench. I let her think it, because to explain the pointless always has a flavor of discourtesy. I thanked her, paid what I had to pay, and went home.

"Ida?" my mother's voice met me.

"I brought lunch," I answered, soothing her anxiety and anticipating the question about where I had been.

We had an almost lighthearted meal, comforted by the television, tuned to the news of the day, and by our scattered comments: the problem of garbage disposal in Rome, the death of a beloved singer of the seventies, the return to Italy of a chef who had become famous in the United States. More than once I had the temptation to stop and tell her that I had met Sara or that Pietro would arrive in a few days, but I didn't want to open between us pathways that I wouldn't have the courage to pursue to the end.

The House of the Puparo

A little before five I began to wonder how Nikos and I would be able to keep our appointment; he would never come down—ringing the bell would mean violating an implicit pact of reserve in front of my mother. I hadn't shown the same tact going up to the roof to demand his presence in front of his father. What to do, then? Go up and once more display the urge to see him, extort my promise?

I looked at myself in the mirror again and saw the same face as in the morning, worn out and slightly depleted, but if I merely thought ahead to the moment when we would be alone my expression lit up. I put a cotton sweater on over the tank top, anticipating the cool of the evening, grabbed my purse, and as soon as I went out ran into Nikos, coming down the stairs to my door. Surprised by that unplanned encounter, we both laughed naturally.

"All right?" he asked me, and we had already gone down the stairs, we had already gone out the entrance door, we were already in front of his motorbike; so I fastened the helmet under my chin and held onto his back to steady myself, hoping that he would take me to the coast. Instead he headed toward the center, and I was disappointed.

We went along the streets parallel to the harbor, following the outline of a cruise ship that looked as if it had been parked amid the buildings of the fortifications, passed by the center, and turned onto Via Industriale, entering the area called Maregrosso. Then I guessed where he wanted to take me and a secure happiness arose inside me, because I, too, loved that place. I'd been there twice in high school, with Sara, and the second time it was dark: we'd gone on a motorbike, and, defying fear, had smoked some grass and gotten lost in the fantasies of that narrow alleyway.

When Nikos and I stopped in front of the house of the man who had been known in the city as Cavaliere Cammarata, or the Puparo, I wondered why, proposing this meeting, he had used the verb "show": "I'll show you something," he had said. Did he really think I had never been there—was I, in his view, so little acquainted with the city? Before us, sparkling and archaic, rose the illegal shanty that Giovanni Cammarata had transformed into a castle, anticipating the art of recycling. He had created mosaics, sculptures, and artistic stained-glass windows using pieces of glass and stone in every shade of every color, alternating figures and abstract designs. This man had made his house a sanctuary or a museum, and until his death had devoted himself to producing beauty on the worst strip of a disintegrating neighborhood.

"You know there were other works here and to make room

for a superstore parking lot they knocked them all down, right?" I started off by letting Nikos understand how close to my heart that place was. "He wanted to create a street of the Arts, with a capital A."

Between us there was an uneasy complicity. I thought of how much Cammarata, a bricklayer with an adventurous life, occupying land not his own and building his universe on it, might excite the mind of a boy who, growing up, had inherited his father's trade and compared it with the Puparo's: the same activity, building houses, took opposite directions—his father obeyed the rules, Cammarata invented them. In between that two-faced model was Nikos. And if by day he worked on the roof of my house, now he was ready to celebrate that achievement of living, anarchic art which constituted another house, ruined and uninhabited. My thoughts and his were so close that there was no need to exchange them.

"I don't know how to build anything beautiful, I'm completely incapable," I said, squatting on the sidewalk at the foot of the motorbike, where Nikos joined me, taking a bag out of the trunk. It contained a plastic bottle filled with a red liquid and two glasses wrapped in newspaper.

"Wine from Etna. You drink?"

He knew that I would drink and that I would prefer a glass to plastic, or maybe he wanted to exhibit a refinement in his manners, make an impression. I crossed my legs, trying to assume a relaxed, casual position. The wine was good, strong: peasant wine.

"I'm sorry about the question I asked yesterday. I usually don't invade people's lives like that."

I felt my knees loosen, the effect of the wine, or of my words.

"It's a terrible story."

"I have strong shoulders."

"It happened two years ago. You want some more?"

We filled the glasses again. I thought it would be nice to have some French fries, something fresh and fragrant; meanwhile Cavaliere Cammarata's dark creatures, their outlines obscured, stared at us in silence. Horses, princes, warriors in armor: we had summoned them all to our hearth.

"Her name is Anna. She's the only girl I've loved. We were coming back together from an afternoon at San Saba, where the mountains of sand are, you know it?"

San Saba, Acqualadroni: they were places I knew well, villages where as a child I went swimming with my father and mother; the beach Nikos referred to was known for its hills of fine, shining sand.

"We'd gone there to swim, that's all. That afternoon we just wanted to talk. Anna had finished school and wanted to enroll in the university, but her parents were against it, they said they didn't have the money, it was just a waste, and anyway she wasn't good at anything, she didn't like studying, and so what had she got it into her head to do."

"And was it true?"

"She had graduated with a low grade and the teachers didn't like her, because she was beautiful and then because she always had an answer. She was 'na rispustera, she'd talk back. She couldn't sit still at a desk, she couldn't be quiet even when she should be."

"She was your girl?"

"She was the girl of a friend of mine," he answered. "It happens."

I said nothing. I drank the second glass of Etna red, holding it tight with two hands as if it were a cup.

"That afternoon we didn't talk about that," he continued. "It had been going on for four months and every day we asked ourselves what to do and how to tell him. She was unsure because she was with him, and was afraid that if she left him he'd kill himself."

"And was that true?"

"I was worried, too. Marcello had a difficult situation at home, his father had died the year before, and he sold drugs. I hang around with people like that, not young ladies, I'm sorry."

"If anything I'm a lady, I'm married."

"You're right."

Nikos poured the third glass of wine and lit a cigarette.

"You're not going to continue?" I urged him.

"I wanted to see if you're bored. I was saying, that day Anna and I hadn't talked about our problems. Anyway they were always the same: we made love every time we saw each other, I wanted her all to myself, she was terrified of leaving him, I felt guilty, she felt guilty, we all felt guilty, except for Marcello, who didn't know anything. That day we had decided not to talk about those things, partly because we'd end up shouting or fighting and there's nothing worse after you've made love."

"How old were you?"

"Eighteen, and she twenty. We had decided to go swimming like a normal couple, as if we were together. We always saw each other secretly, never in a pizzeria, very seldom at the café, she had this nightmare that someone might see us and tell Marcello. So I proposed: Let's do a normal thing. Let's go out. Let's go swimming. The sea helps you think."

"I also do that, but I have to be alone. If you swim with someone it's not the same."

"That day it worked. Anna was gorgeous in her bathing suit. Dressed or naked, yes, but I'd never seen her in a bathing suit. She'd put on a black bathing suit, she was all white, with hair blacker than yours, wet after swimming. Everybody looked at her. If I had been her boyfriend I would have been proud, and I did feel proud, because I was her boyfriend. She didn't love Marcello anymore."

I would have liked to tell him none of us know whom we really love, and there are so many different things inside the word "love" that at twenty you shouldn't name it, but this was the thought of an old woman and I kept it to myself.

"She hadn't brought another suit to change into. So she put her shirt on over the wet one and took it off underneath, then she put on her pants, and she got on the motorbike, pants and shirt and naked underneath."

"You'd been swimming?"

"Far out, and I had kissed her, in the water and out of the water, I was mad for Anna. We practically did it on the beach in front of everyone."

"When did it happen?" I asked in a faint voice.

"Coming home. A car passed us on a curve. I watched her die in front of me."

The Puparo's warriors stared at us, with their mixture of magic and seduction. That was what Nikos wanted to show me: not a physical place but the terrible place that was his life.

"I dream about her as if she were still with me, she looks at me, she says nothing, in the shadow there's only her figure. Sometimes she moves her mouth to talk to me but her voice doesn't come out. But I know what she would say: she won't forgive me because I killed her."

"But it wasn't your fault," I said right away, to protect him.

"According to the law, no, but I don't give a shit about the law, even though she was wearing a helmet, even though I was going slowly, and even though we were in the right. At the funeral Marcello was crying; because I'm no one, I couldn't even go to the church. Anna's parents hated him, they knew he sold drugs, what sort of life he had, but death changes things, after the accident he became the best guy in the world, while who'd want to see me, even if it wasn't my fault. Then Marcello also changed for real, poor guy, he's not on the street now, and works in a computer store. He's not a bad kid. Whereas I had broken my ribs and they wouldn't let me out of the hospital, I cursed the nurses to their faces and the more I yelled the more they forced me to sleep. You know how I lived? Think of this sensation: as if I'd been tied up in a garbage bag. A black bag, thrown into a bin. I deserved it." He put out the cigarette. "I deserve it."

I knew that bag. The bag in which the body of a woman or a mannequin had been cut into pieces in one of my latest nightmares. The plastic bag around my neck that might strangle me any day, tighten over me, cutting off the air, that bag full of old things I had just thrown away. I squeezed Nikos's arm, he placed a hand on mine. I couldn't read the block letters above a scene drawn by the Puparo; time had erased some of the lines, and I didn't feel like getting up, moving away from the warmth of the shoulder of that young man overwhelmed by unhappiness and regret. We sat close together and talked, not looking at each other, both staring at the creatures before us.

"It was the greatest love in the world. There won't ever be another love like that. I would have married her. I would never have left her. If only she could have convinced herself, right now we'd be happy. I've been with a lot of girls but no one was Anna, I felt at home with her, we were equals, two strong people who didn't want to yield."

"But even if you and she had been together, she still would have died."

I, too, got stuck in his hypotheses: if Anna had left Marcello, if on that day they had been engaged, not secret lovers, if their bond had been official . . . It was absurd, senseless. But these hypotheses were all he had; he had brought me there to tell them to me, in a place that was dear to him and dear to me, a place that few Messinese knew and still fewer frequented: at night it became a rough, criminal alleyway, by day the customers of the superstore never suspected how much beauty might radiate from this place, maybe they even took the liberty of a vulgar gibe, mocking the project of a man who couldn't be categorized. Whereas Nikos and I, very different in age and experience, had nourished ourselves on the folly of the Puparo, had accepted it as our frame.

"How many people know this story?" was my last question.

"Only strangers. The only ones you can tell things to."

When Nikos brought me home, I simply felt grateful.

Eighth Nocturne

Nothing to do about it, impossible to sleep.

I have to wait for dawn, guided by the clamor of horses like the ones in the clandestine races that kept me awake as a child and still take place: just a few months ago my husband pointed out that there are videos on the Internet—proud bettors, mafiosi shouts and cheers, animals cut down by a sudden collapse on the asphalt. The inferno, a few steps from my house.

No, impossible to sleep.

Concentric circles of stories hold me in a false embrace. Sleep is impossible when memory is an open storehouse and every detail is looking for a place in a story.

My mind needs to rest, but it can't, because today other people's suffering displaced mine, and while I'm used to mine, this I don't know how to handle, and first of all I would like to ask if it has always existed or decided to visit me all at once just now. Sara's cancer operation after the abortion, the sentence she received, to be unable to choose whether to have a biological child or not, her coldness toward me because growing up means knowing whom you can do without. Nikos's scar, Nikos who carries on his shoulders the death of the beloved the way the old mules of Pantelleria carried travelers' suitcases across the island. Impossible to sleep, because the scenes are strung together and now it's up to me to be silent and observe that assembly line. "I deserve it," Nikos said of his sense of guilt. I understand, I know what it means; "I don't deserve it," I say of the sleep of the just, which doesn't arrive and which I'm not entitled to. Impossible to sleep, because I've wasted time, a prisoner of myself, barricaded by fear. Yes, my obsessions, yes, the alarm clock stopped at six-sixteen, the trail of toothpaste like the slimy trail of a snail, yes, all right: but while my father performed for me, other suffering played in other places, all at the same time, evil continues to exist while we're busy thinking of ourselves; people die, get sick, suffer, seek, seek you, don't find.

Impossible to sleep, and it's better to get up and look for an answer to the voices that assail me. "Subsume" would be the right verb: take upon myself the lives of others. I'm not capable of doing it with the living, maybe I can succeed with the dead, but what's truly urgent is to think of the survivors. How does Nikos live, who loved Anna until a moment before her last breath? He still does, he continued, to stop loving someone is not among the collateral effects of death. One goes on feeling desire: not affection but pure yearning: Nikos carried it in his gaze as he spoke and recounted, desire deposited in the details he insistently paused on, the bathing suit, the shorts, the wet hair. No, one doesn't stop loving someone because she's not there: if it's valid for parents, siblings, friends, why shouldn't it be the same for boy- or girlfriends, spouses, lovers? Desire doesn't succumb.

Nikos desired Anna, we all desire someone who has left us, would we like to have a glass of wine with him one last time at a table on a narrow street, ask again the questions we've already asked, give in to the warmth, the embraces, a lost fragrance, spiky and familiar, just as it appears to us in dreams because it couldn't happen in reality? Once, just once.

Impossible to sleep, my head is bursting.

I get up: I know exactly what I'm looking for: my red iron box.

For twenty-three years it's been shut in a drawer, not even my mother suspects its existence. I've kept it secret, thinking that one day I would be ready to open it, and in order to put that box in a safe place I crossed Italy and the Strait, endured the September smog and the plaster dust; when my mother said on the telephone that I had to choose what to keep and what to throw away I was afraid it would be thrown away, when she said she had rummaged among the objects I was afraid she'd found it, tossed it away carelessly, as a thing without importance, or with determination, so that the past wouldn't return to infect her hands. No, one doesn't stop loving someone when his name and his body are removed: we carry the voice and odor of the absent one, the two most unstable traces; we'd recognize them anywhere, and every so often we seem to hear them, and then we're affectionate toward what has reminded us of them, a space or a person or a sound. My father's odor of tobacco and his nasal and imperious voice had accompanied me everywhere I went in the past twenty-three years, and sometimes it seemed to me that I grasped them, but that was always followed by a sense of defeat.

But now sleep is impossible, the moment has arrived.

I get up from the bed and go to the desk, I open the fourth drawer, the bottom, the lowest. I move a packet of letters, Sara's letters, from the time when we wrote to each other with a green pen and in the morning exchanged densely written sheets of perfumed paper. I also move aside a notebook and two diaries: the red metal box is where it's always been.

I hold it, I observe it, I study it, and I recognize it. Twenty-three years ago I put in here the proofs of the existence of a man named Sebastiano Laquidara, in this red box I buried the smell and the voice of my father.

With a small snap I force the opening. The tobacco in the pipe nestled on the bottom rises to my nostrils, goes down my throat; I close my eyes and enjoy as an adult the scent of my childhood. There it is, the aroma that followed my father when he went in and out of rooms, that remained stuck to cheeks and neck after kisses and cuddles. I sniff the air and find who I was, sniff and know who I am. I move the pipe from one hand to the other, hold it in my fingers, caress it and bring it to my nostrils, I let that smell release its power, exerting absolute control over me until the feeling becomes too much, and I have to get away; as I move toward the balcony the smell fades and almost vanishes, I go back, I'm crying, finally I cry.

I cry as long as I have tears, while I'm waiting to move on to the second object placed on the bottom of the box, a cassette in its plastic case, my mother's handwriting on lined paper: "Ida at 11." I can't keep the memories in order, one prevails: the day of my birthday I had an outfit—flowered sweater and skirt, pale wool stockings, black shoes tied with a small loop, why should a child wear black shoes, what evil omen is that heel of a future Achilles?—I blew out eleven pink candles right there, in the living room, the cake was a profiterole (in our house we called it "white and black," good and evil). I had had eleven candles and a few presents, a pair of new skates from my father, my hair pulled back in a braid by my mother, children around, childhood friends whose names I don't remember, but I remember the three of us: my father my mother and me, the original triangle. I blow out the candles, the children leave, my mother urges, Let's sing, I dance, I jump on the couch with my shoes, no one scolds me, my parents have drunk spumante, they've drunk too much. My mother doesn't sing, she leaves the room, returns with the stereo, takes the wrapping off a new cassette, presses the key REC, the memory breaks off. Darkness.

Two years passed, and in that time my father's body disappeared, while his imprint remained in the house, his absence the first damp stain on the ceiling, and my mother and I are alone, nothing but alone. My father has left us, we didn't fight hard enough, we're unworthy of him and a good fate, we made a mistake, we failed, we're condemned, we're rejected. My father's name has disappeared, I'm about to be defeated, I squeeze my palms and no longer find anything to squeeze. It's November 2nd when I reckon with my blood: my first period arrives the morning of the Day of the Dead. It was late and here it is, my father disappeared and I have to grow up, menstruation says I've already grown up. I come out of the bathroom frightened by a transformation I can't oppose, at all costs I have to hold on to my father, how can I hold on to my father who's leaving? His body disappears from the shirts hanging on the hangers, his hands disappear from mine, my father's no longer here, my mother's at the museum, I run to his room, to their room, I open the drawers of the night table, in the first my mother's things, in the second my father's, I steal the pipe from among the objects belonging to him, I steal the tape from hers, I carry them off to safety in my room, those two objects alone matter to me, I choose a box to put them in, I choose a drawer to bury them in. The pipe and the tape recording, and that's all. Everywhere, inside and outside the house, my father's name is disappearing, along with his body, but thanks to me his smell and his voice are safe.

Twenty-three years have passed since that November 2nd. Two hundred and eighty menstrual cycles, and today I'm defenseless before the red box; it's night and I've given up sleeping, I've put the pipe back, but the smell of tobacco lingers in the room. It's the tape's turn, who listens to cassettes anymore? Among the objects to keep or throw away is the stereo of my adolescence. Now, twenty-three years later, the stereo will restore my father's voice.

I take the tape out of the case, "Ida at 11," and put it in the player, PLAY. I wait.

It begins with a rustling, with my mother's voice in the middle of a word: ". . . ing because we're recording, Ida, speak here!" (What was the word? speak-ing, look-ing, sing-ing?) The voice scratches and exults from another era. I never heard it that way again, it was my father's presence hidden amid the sharp sounds, the laughter, that made it strong: "Sebastiano, say something to us!" There was my mother just as I'd known her: a frightening and elusive woman who gives orders, who rules without ever getting her hands dirty. I never really thought of her suffering, I recognize it now by what's been removed, while I seek to reconstruct what she had and no longer does. "Papa, talk here, talk": what a grotesque child's voice I had, the voice of a gnome or a creature of the understory, and a nasal laugh, like a dinosaur, a laugh bigger than me. It must have been the year when, skating near the sea without the encumbrance of my coat, I had been in danger of getting sick, and my mother had reproached my father for his rashness: You were supposed to put the scarf on her and instead you let her take off what she had on. She spoke to him in that very voice, the same one I hear now. The tape continues, and finally a man arrives, whispering. It's very strange: I didn't remember anyone else there, apart from my father.

"Sebastiano, come on, sing!" my mother interjects again.

I can't believe it, I press STOP. For twenty-three years I've waited to hear my father's voice again, and when I do I don't recognize it.

I want to rewind and go back, but I'm afraid of damaging the tape, and if it breaks?

Maybe back just to that voice that I need to hear again, that I have to regain possession of. Better to wait, better to put it off, onward.

PLAY, again.

Tape, please: don't break, don't break off.

Meanwhile my father obeys and begins to sing softly,

his thin voice grows large, powerful, luminous, and I start laughing, and I laugh and laugh.

He sings, and sings, and sings. The room fills with his name, his body, his voice, and his smell, and night envelops the Strait and the whole city of Messina, night envelops my father's disappearance, my mother's cassette, my laughter, tears, and whatever up to that moment has passed over the Earth.

The Unfinished Sadness

The iced coffee at the café mingled with the taste of the warm brioche, just out of the oven, and the spoonful of whipped cream on the coffee. My mother, with a mulberry and pistachio granita in front of her, was intent on dunking her brioche in it.

"You start with the hat?" I teased her. The hat was the top part of the brioche, the most fragrant piece, which she and my father had taught me to save for last, to enjoy in a single final mouthful, like a reward.

"You're boring, Ida. Why do you always have to criticize everything?"

"I didn't sleep well. Really I didn't sleep at all."

At seven I'd gone into the kitchen, my mother was making coffee, and I had proposed that we go out instead, have breakfast out.

I wanted to tell her about the night, tell her about my father's voice, hers and mine that were blurred together, about that ridiculous detail: that I hadn't recognized it right away. Share the discovery that the obsession that had taken shape in my head was so compact and autonomous that at some point it had become untethered from reality: my father's voice didn't resemble my memory of it at all.

"I, on the other hand, slept right through. You could have called me, I wouldn't have heard you. Did you read?" she asked, distracted.

"More or less."

I swallowed the last sip of coffee and licked the edge of the glass. Sicilian whipped cream had a special taste, a non-taste that distinguished it from whipped cream in the rest of Italy, always sugary or invasive. Here it wasn't too sweet or too liquid or too artificial. I looked finally at the hat of my brioche, but my mother, playing a trick, stole it from me and bit into it right before my astonished eyes.

"That'll teach you to leave the best for last."

"You and Papa taught me!"

"Children need to learn patience, for adults there's no point in knowing how to wait."

Life is *ein Augenblick*, the child my mother spoke of no longer existed, the new adult who had replaced her needed a new sentimental education. There were many things I would be able to get rid of, starting with that verb: "Wait."

We got up to go home and decided to see how the De Salvos were doing on the roof, but my mother stopped downstairs to get the list of what was left to be done before the work could be considered finished. On the roof there was no one.

I took out of the pocket of my shorts a piece of paper I'd found in the drawer the night before, in the pile of papers that covered the red box. In the handwriting of my university days, I had copied down a poem by Amelia Rosselli.

> *If the weeping that yields to regret*
> *yields to me its lute,*
> *I can make these slow beaches*
> *the imminent reach*
> *of unfinished sadness**

I connected those words to Nikos.

The night before had left me with confused thoughts and violent emotions, a mixture of respect for and fear of his terrible story, and yet he had told it with simplicity. I wondered how he had found the strength to confront the suffering, and especially the impossibility of expressing it legitimately: Anna was someone else's girlfriend, not his. He was only the witness of an accident that, no matter what the law said, he would continue to feel guilty for. He was the survivor of a secret love, and would have to carry its weight, counting the years to come without her. As for Anna, going with Nikos and Marcello at the same time, she must have put off the choice, imagining that she had before her an unlimited calendar, that she could enjoy the time she needed to put things in place; but life is *ein Augenblick*, irregularity is its only rule, events roll past us while we have the illusion that one day we'll control them. That was why I took refuge in my fake true stories: over them I exercised absolute sovereignty. I was the ruler of what I

---

* Amelia Rosselli, *Appunti sparsi e persi. 1966–1977.* (Rome: Edizioni Empiria, 1997).

wrote; I constructed characters and moved them around, I recorded their complaints, their priorities, their satisfactions, like a god or a despot. Writing, I had the illusion of being self-sufficient.

As in a game of crisscrossing memories, I went from the conversation with Nikos to the last phone call with Pietro, asking myself what I could have done to shift some of the omnipotence of my writing to choices I'd made, imagining myself and those around me as characters in one of my stories: Pietro and I had fallen, yes, but we had fallen together—maybe if we held each other by the hand we could rise again? But broken things, *spasciate*, the Messinese would have said in dialect, can't be repaired.

I was relieved to hear heavy, rapid footsteps: the De Salvos, late, would begin a new day of work.

But my mother emerged from the stairway instead, agitated.

She ran toward me, hugged me, wept.

"Nikos is dead," she said.

I thought it was a joke, that an intelligent adult woman like her shouldn't believe it.

I thought there was a mistake, they were mistaken, who knows whom they were talking about, she had misunderstood.

I thought of a case of someone with the same name.

I thought that it couldn't happen to me. That was how I thought of it: as a thing that had happened to me, not to him.

And my mother and I became what we had always been: two women, dismayed, on the damaged roof of a house that was too big, lost amid an unfinished job and an unfinished sadness, one facing the other and both facing an abandonment.

Farewell

Sitting among the people who filled the cathedral, I noticed that the bell tower didn't sound, nothing sounded, not the Schubert "Ave Maria" or the roars of the mechanical clock, in the air was the hum of people crowding to a funeral. Only two days before I'd wanted to go to that square to recover memories of adolescence; now there were no more memories, they had been supplanted by a crowd that crushed and wept, a crowd that didn't want to believe the unbelievable, a young man of twenty who had killed himself, and out of compassion it skipped over the details, but I knew that he had hanged himself, like my father in the first dream I'd had about him, with a sheet around the neck, and that no one had been able to prevent him. Looking at the scene now with the distance that time provides, I see my mother and me—in the midst of that crowd that talks and knows and doesn't want to know—as lost figures, arms linked, and even today I struggle to focus on our first gestures; the tears, the condolences, the incredulity aren't real; the priest who invites Nikos's sister to the pulpit is real, and she, stumbling as she goes up, is real. The scene is in the present tense, the tense of nightmares, of insomnia, of obsessions, the eternal tense that the past crowds into.

I observe my last day in Messina from a distant point.

In the girl with proud eyes who struggles to read from a piece of paper full of memories and words of love written in pen I perceive Nikos's voice, when he told me about her, about his mother, about Crete and sadness, and I hear him silent about his scar. His little sister wears eyeglasses and weeps as she reads, her cheeks are newly furrowed, she wears a black shirt, a black skirt, black shoes. She has words of love and torment for her brother that I can't take in. The time of a funeral is removed from real time: when it takes place the person is still there, the imprint of what he was is so recent, and our mind struggles to understand. I keep my eyes fixed on the wooden coffin because Nikos might wake, knock, and legitimately demand to come out: You're crazy to have closed me up in here, I'm suffocating, what did you think, what have you done. I can't take my eyes off the flower-covered coffin even for an instant, it will be up to me to register the thud, the fist beating from within, the muffled cries and the desire for air and justice, I'll have to rush to open it when Nikos returns.

My mother next to me is crying. "He was such a handsome boy, he was a boy," she sobs. "It's not just, it's not right," she insists, and looks for my hand. I would like to say something, but I don't know how. At least give her some support, but I don't even know how to do that, while in a single sentence she talks about Nikos, whom she knew for a few days, and my father, whom she slept with for two decades, making no distinction between them: she speaks the way my mother speaks, not getting to the heart of things but spinning beside them in a rage.

We're close, finally at a funeral.

My mother and I can now say farewell to someone, and by means of a boy we also say goodbye to that other who was once a boy; but there is no trace of my father in the church or outside, in the bells or the sound of the organ, he's absent from the naves, from among Nikos's schoolmates, from among his family, the Sicilians who live here and the Greeks who've come from the other side of the sea, summoned by the catastrophe. My father is set aside: it's not him we weep for today, if anything we weep for not having wept for him and we steal a piece of suffering that has nothing to do with us, awkward in our dark dresses.

Where was I the other night, after saying goodbye to Nikos? Could I have kept him from killing himself? Perceived in his confession in front of the house of the Puparo the trace of a will? No answer can soothe the survivors. There's a closet full of answers that the living try on depending on the day, there is the answer that Nikos couldn't give himself, persecuted by the idea that he'd lost salvation around a bend in a road: in the life that didn't happen, Anna would have found the strength to leave Marcello, she would have returned to him to put on a hundred black bathing suits, and they would have kissed each other on a hundred thousand beaches with mountains of sand behind them. But there is no parallel life, anywhere, nothing exists except what has existed, and surely count-less times Nikos's mind had been deluded and got stuck on the same scene: kisses, swims, shorts, motorcycle. He had become a survivor and would remain one until death: impatient, he had wanted to shorten the time that separated him from the end. No one is alive: all of us are only—*still* alive. We live in the time of "for now."

The young men who carry the coffin on their shoulders walk with cold composure, I understand they are under-takers when I hear the whisper of two men in the square: We should have done it. Then I seem to recognize in them a cousin, an uncle; the faces of relatives always seem a rough copy of the person we knew, touched. I recall my father's mother, who died when I was a small child, the grand-mother who kept me with her in the big bed and urged me to recount my nightmares: hearing my father say Mamma to that woman with the complexion similar to his, the same nose, elongated eyes gave me the impression of a distorting mirror (it was partly the effect of seeing the father become a son again: five letters, his first word, "mamma").

But Nikos's mother doesn't resemble him, she's short and round, she has curly hair, flabby arms. I get in the line for condolences and when it's my turn I hug Signor De Salvo, I turn to the wife, I take her hands, I'm Ida Laquidara, I say, and she nods her head yes, Nikos was working on the roof of my house, I add, and holding her it seems to me I'm holding her son and I don't want to stop, I raise her forearms, kiss her hands in an ancient gesture.

The last person I see is the sister, standing still in the square, in the center of a million people, small and solid as a lemon tree; then the coffin is in the car and the De Salvo family is gone.

My mother and I don't linger. When the car with Nikos's body disappears, we go back to being strangers to ourselves and the crowd, the rite is over, the present time is over; turning our backs to the cathedral, we leave the dream that we never wanted to have, and the outlines of the houses assume the features of reality.

Then my mother and I walked along Via Cavour, and without saying a word we passed shops and food stores, cafés and the classical high school, where she had gone, and the perpendicular street that leads to the other high school, where I had gone, and, still silent, we crossed Torrente Boccetta and entered Villa Mazzini: the pond where swans once swam was full of floating cigarette butts and wet leaves. And again we passed by the *Ficus macrophylla*, the witches' tree that I had seen the same and different in Palermo, in Piazza Marina: I greeted it with a nod of the head and a leap of the heart, as I would have greeted an old friend who had come to bring me comfort after a stormy night.

Finally, outside the villa, in front of the fountain of Neptune that welcomed sailors, I asked my mother a question.

"What will you do about the roof?"

"The important thing is that the De Salvos had installed the insulation. Maybe it will fall on my head, never mind. I still have in my ears Nikos's voice, every time I had a doubt: Signora, I know you want to sell, but let's say you don't sell, at least you'll find the lamps in place. He didn't believe I would sell, and so, well, all right: I'll keep it like that, as I've always kept it. And when I die you can decide."

A hint of sirocco was blowing, and I felt the sweat on my back; in my mind were the words of the priest in the cathedral, eternal life and union with the Father, the angels, and the family, for whom, he said, the boy would continue to live, as he would in the hearts of good people. I didn't have faith. I didn't want people to live in the hearts of others—I wanted them to live in the world with me, and so I would miss Nikos, whom I'd just met, forever.

"You were alike: vagabond children, never content. But he was so young compared to you, and weren't you fond of him? I thought right away you'd be friends."

"He's sixteen years younger. Was, I mean," I concluded, as if that past tense were important. I would never talk to my mother about the evening at the Puparo, would never tell her that I knew the story of the scar on his left cheekbone, which even she might have noticed. I would never recount the lives of Anna and Nikos to her or to my husband: that country boy's candid, wine-washed dialogue was like another red box that I would keep for myself. I had become a witness, a survivor in my turn: Anna and Nikos would die with me.

"Shall we have lunch at that new place, in Muricello?" I suggested. A blue-and-white restaurant had opened, with a marine décor reminiscent of boats; I was curious to go there, and didn't want to go home right away. I didn't feel like cooking or bothering with setting the table and clearing it. My mother agreed. A polite host welcomed us, and we ordered calamari and caponata, mussels and spaghetti in a stockfish sauce *a' ghiotta*, with tomatoes, olives, and capers; I had a glass of red wine, which she looked at disapprovingly.

"Since when do you drink at lunch?"

"Just today."

It was a lunch with some laughter, as lunches tend to be after funerals, when we laugh with the chill of death still upon us, imagining that the deceased would have laughed with us, and maybe at us. I thought that Nikos would have tugged on the sleeve of the shirt I was wearing and ordered me to stop being sad. I cried a little, as nervously as I'd laughed, and my mother held my hand on the table, as I had been unable to hold hers. Then she recounted anecdotes from her childhood: a doll she had loved very much but had had to throw away because another girl, the child of neighbors, had carried it up on a high sofa and gouged out its eyes to spite her.

"That doll was too beautiful, the doll Silvana," she sighed.

"You remember the names of your dolls?"

"Also of yours. Teresa, that's the name of the one you still have in your room."

"I've got a lot, and I don't play with any of them anymore."

"Choose what to keep—it's why I asked you to come. Even if I'm not going to sell, it's a chance to organize."

"Go through my stuff, I give you permission. You want to know who your daughter is? Here's your opportunity. Choose, throw away, *scartafruscia, scafulía*. You see, now that I'm leaving, dialect comes to me. You can read my diaries, assuming you haven't already. The letters Sara wrote me. You can choose to read nothing and get rid of it all. Even the dolls, do what you want with them."

My mother didn't answer; besides, what I'd said to her wasn't, this time, in the form of a question. I didn't leave room for a response.

"Pietro's coming to get me in Villa San Giovanni."

"I'll go with you."

"You don't have to. The crossing is mine, it's the thing I have that's most mine—I want to do it alone. Let's go home, I'll get my suitcase and go. Mamma, if you can't sleep tonight call me."

"All right," she said, and the rest was lost in goodbyes.

There's a final scene that repeats eternally in the present, at the end of nightmares, insomnias, obsessions, and a funeral. Even today I don't know if it's true or if I dreamed it, just as I don't know if the objects that animate it existed or if Ida Laquidara is really the woman on the ferry that is heading away from the island, away from the house with the crumbling roof, away from the mother and the absence of the father, away from the despair and death of a young man of twenty.

It's getting dark: the Sicilian coast is growing dim, the Madonna of the harbor blesses the sailors, the buildings fade, and in a corner of the view the house between the two seas is visible, too. I lean over the parapet for a last goodbye and another crossing comes to mind, made up of discussions of dolphins and first cigarettes and icy beers, the day of adolescence when I went to Scylla, and would return after losing my body or maybe after having exercised the greatest possible control over it.

At the time I talked nervously, eager to seem someone, while on this new crossing I do nothing: I observe, and the strangers appear to me as what they are, what we are, a group of survivors each of his own battle. I see a multitude of men and women and children all missing families, friends, lovers; I see crowds of people who have passed through death and emerged damaged, disturbed, but the same. We're all coming from a funeral, not only I who was at one in fact; we've all lost someone and we know how long and unjust the time before us is, the time without that person. The time that we begin to count year by year, starting from the loss.

I don't know much about the lives of others, but if I opened my solitude just a crack it would become crowded.

Maybe tomorrow I'll be ready to open my door. Not now. Now I'm looking.

I look at people: some smoking, some eating rice balls, some watching out for their children and some thinking about the journey, whether it's a return or a departure. Maybe, in order to know whether I'm returning or leaving on this crossing that I've made thousands of times, I have to ask myself if my back is turned or my eyes are on my house: there's only one for every life, as in the wisdom of his twenty years Nikos pointed out to me. Many are the houses that we can inhabit, but only one lights up when we hear the word *house*. *House*, I repeat to myself, and I turn toward the continent and Rome, which awaits me; *house*, I repeat, now with my gaze on the island and Messina, which is saying farewell. My house is neither of the two, it's in the middle of two seas and two lands. My house is here, now.

Decisively, and with quick fingers, I look for the zipper of my suitcase, open it, take out the red iron box. With both hands, as if it were the wine glass offered in front of the ruined castle of the Puparo, I hold it tight for a final farewell and throw it into the water, which welcomes it.

The voice and smell of my father, which I shut up and saved for twenty-three years, from this moment will have their tomb on the bottom of the Strait. They will be swallowed by the fish or by Charybdis rising to the surface for the occasion, or they'll remain stuck in the scales of Homer's Sirens: I will be far away, and my theater will remain empty.

Thus my father exits the scene.

So I laugh, turning toward both coasts like a two-faced goddess, between the island and the land, standing on the ship in the midst of people who don't see me, because they're bent over their telephones or distracted, their dim gaze on thoughts that don't concern me.

I laugh and laugh. I laugh, and an epoch ends in the sound of a dive, in the sea that opens and swallows up without giving back. I laugh and laugh again, before a tomb that only I know; and at last the small watch on my wrist says six-seventeen.

Born in Messina, Sicily, NADIA TERRANOVA is the author of *Gli anni al contrario*; *Casca il mondo*; *Bruno, il bambino che imparò a volare*; and *Addio Fantasmi* (*Farewell, Ghosts*). She also writes for the Italian newspaper *La Repubblica*. *Farewell, Ghosts* is her first book to be published in English.

Translator ANN GOLDSTEIN is a former editor at *The New Yorker*. She has translated works by, among others, Primo Levi, Pier Paolo Pasolini, Elena Ferrante, Italo Calvino, and Alessandro Baricco, and is the editor of *The Complete Works of Primo Levi* in English. She has been the recipient of a Guggenheim fellowship and awards from the Italian Ministry of Foreign Affairs and the American Academy of Arts and Letters.